NORTH POLE UNLIMITED COLLECTION 3

BEN AND JILLY, FRANK AND GINGER

ELLE RUSH

SBD ENTERTAINMENT

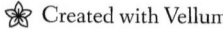

ACKNOWLEDGEMENTS AND DEDICATIONS

This book is dedicated to the one I love. Thanks, Ross, for being the person who would save me if I ever threatened to become the Grinch.

Special thanks to Ali B. for suggesting the name for Ben's dog in my newsletter contest. It was so close to the "Spirit" of Christmas that I couldn't resist.

My appreciation to the amazing people who helped on this book, my editor Dayna Hart and proofreader Kim Cannon.

And thank you to all my supportive writing friends: Susan Hayes, Melanie Ting, Sidney Bristol, Megan Matthews, Jenn Fischetto, Susan Saxx, Kate Willoughby, L.C. Allenye.

BEN AND JILLY

A North Pole Unlimited Romance
By
Elle Rush

BLURB

When North Pole Unlimited's #1 elf turns Scrooge, a new flame and his furry sidekick need to jumpstart her Christmas spirit before it's too late.

Executive assistant Jilly Lewis has never resented Christmas before, but this year, the company's resident matchmaker and holiday disaster-fixer has learned her family is going to be elsewhere during the most wonderful time of the year.

Ebenezer "Ben" Fredericks is giving up the road for a desk job at North Pole Unlimited. He has lots of things to do as he reorganizes his life in the town of December, but number one on his list is getting Jilly back into the Christmas spirit.

He'll need to enlist help to put the jingle back in Jilly's step, and his new co-workers and neighbours in

December are eager to pay back Jilly for her years of spreading Christmas joy everywhere she goes.

Can Ben put the ho-ho-ho back in Jilly's holidays, or will she find coal in her stocking on Christmas morning? Only Santa knows.

Join Elle Rush's newsletter to keep up with her latest releases and other news.

CHAPTER 1

FIRST WEEK *of December*
   North Pole Unlimited Headquarters
   December, Manitoba, Canada (25 kilometres south-east of Winnipeg)

"Merry freaking Christmas." Jilly Lewis, December's number one Christmas cheerleader, glared when the box, which had been balanced on the arm of the sofa, slipped off and spilled all its ornaments over the cushions. "Bah, humbug."

It didn't matter. Her house was already a disaster. Four containers of holiday decorations littered the beige carpet in her living room, her coffee table was covered with a mess of candles and picture frames, and a massive length of fir branches wound with lights lay in the middle of the hall. Jilly ignored them all as she fought with her dining room table. She'd already removed one leaf, but the second refused to cooperate. The table hadn't been its original size since she'd purchased it twenty-four years earlier because she'd always had a full house for every holiday.

But not this year. This year, everybody had abandoned her. She'd be alone for Christmas. Her dining room would have an echo because it was so empty.

Jilly gave the slat an extra-hard tug, but it didn't budge.

Before she could let loose the frustrated growl building in her throat, a flash of light on the living room wall distracted her. It was immediately followed by the rumble of a massive engine.

Her lonely, terrible night just got a little better.

Squeaks and rattles got louder as she opened her front door and waited for the semi-truck to come to rest. After all the lights were extinguished, a form clambered down and walked around the massive machine. "Is it too late?" a man called from the street.

"Not at all. Come in out of the cold," Jilly said.

When trucker Ebenezer "Ben" Fredericks returned from a trip, he dropped his tractor trailer at the North Pole Unlimited loading docks, and then swung by her house so he could hand over the associated paperwork after hours. It had grown from a "drop and leave" event to her inviting him in for a drink and conversation. It was a tradition now. One that she'd miss, since this was his last run.

"Thank you. The heater in this old beast is acting up, and I'm half-frozen." When he got closer, Jilly saw a few curls of brown hair around the edges of a brown toque, and a hint of white in his brown mustache. She wasn't sure if the white was frost, icing sugar, or Ben's silver fox natural looks coming through.

She hung his quilted plaid jacket on the hook at the

front door, and put the kettle on while he ducked into the bathroom. When he came out, she made sure not to notice how good he looked, with the mature streaks in his slightly-too-long hair, or the crinkles on the edges of his coffee-brown eyes. She certainly didn't comment about how trim he was under his chest-hugging sweater. Because friends didn't notice things like that, and they were friends and nothing more. But one last accidental look wouldn't hurt, for old times' sake. She likely wouldn't see him much at all after he started his new job.

Jilly opened her mouth to invite him to take a seat on the sofa, but it looked like a Christmas bomb had exploded on it. She turned to the dining room, but the table was in pieces. She'd have to clean the kitchen table in order for them to enjoy their cocoa.

"Can I help with this?" Ben asked gesturing at the dining room table.

"The last leaf is stuck. I can't get it out. I'll leave it if you'll help me push the ends back together." It would be depressing to have the big, empty table staring her in the face all month, but she'd learn to live with it.

"Let me try." He leaned over the table and with a single jiggle, pulled the board free. "Where do you want this?"

She pointed to the wall where the other piece stood in the corner. "I must have loosened it for you."

"It was definitely loosened," he agreed with a laugh. He glanced into the kitchen. "You sit, and I'll get the tray."

Jilly slumped in the closest chair, and Ben was back before she got comfortable. He passed her a china mug full of frothy cocoa, set a plate of cookies between them, and sat across the table.

"You're not your usual bubbly self. Rough day?"

"Everybody has abandoned me over the holidays," she blurted. She hadn't told anyone yet, but with Ben the news just came out.

"What?"

"My family has plans elsewhere for Christmas this year. I'm going to be all alone," she wailed. She hadn't ever been alone for the holidays ever.

He pushed the plate closer to her. "Tell me everything."

Jilly picked a candy cane cookie and dunked it in her cocoa. "I'm being ridiculous. December is a busy month for my family this year. My parents are spending three weeks touring Australia to celebrate their fifty-fifth wedding anniversary. My oldest sister and her husband were transferred to England in the fall, and it's too soon for them to come home, even for the holidays. My other sister and her husband are spending Christmas with their daughter and their first grandbaby in Calgary. Which are all good reasons to miss my legendary sage-and-onion stuffing and homemade cranberry sauce, but it sucks that it's all happening at the same time," she sighed. She missed them already, and everybody but one sister was still in town.

"That's a lot, and all of it is exciting. I didn't know you were from a family of globetrotters. You'll be looking at pictures for weeks when they all get back in the new year."

"That's true." But it was a small comfort at the moment.

"What about Dan? He'll be on break from university."

She paused for a moment, reminding herself that Ben

didn't know he was poking at a sore spot. "Dan? My son? The light of my life? He's spending Christmas Day with Alex and his family since I got them for Thanksgiving. They're driving down for Boxing Day, so it's not like I won't see him, it just won't be on the twenty-fifth. This being fair and sharing with family is no fun at all," she whined. Not that she wanted Alex to miss Christmas with his family; she just needed someone to invent a teleporter in the next three weeks.

Ben had the nerve to laugh at her. "You're the one who taught him those terrible habits. Shame on you." He pushed the plate closer. "Have another cookie."

"That's not very sympathetic, Ben." But he'd made her smile, which she hadn't thought was possible. She grabbed another cookie in case he was right.

"I'm glad to see you still plan to deck the halls, though." He studied the boxes and clear plastic bins filled with garland and ornaments strewn around the main floor.

"I'm not. Dan helped me move all the furniture and brought in the decorations from the garage last weekend before he dropped his bomb on me. I haven't worked up the energy to put everything back."

Ben dropped his cherry chocolate chip cookie into his mug. "What do you mean you're not decorating? You always decorate. I've been dropping off my reports for two years and you've never had less than two trees up. Your house is Christmas Central, and that's saying something, considering where we work."

He wasn't wrong. Jilly was proud of the festive displays she put together each year. She had enough variety that she could mix and match a dozen themes to keep everything fresh. "I'll put a little sign in the window telling people Whoville is closed for the season." She didn't have any motivation to do all that work, not when there wouldn't be anyone around to enjoy it. The mantle could stay bare; she didn't need the increase to her electricity bill with all the lights she'd have to plug in. Jilly reached for another cookie. She didn't have the heart to *decorate*. She'd be fine with Christmas baking. "Can we change the subject? How was your run?"

Ben fished the cookie out of the bottom of his mug. "Good," he said. "I came through Minnesota on the way home from Chicago and got rerouted because of an accident. I stumbled across a cute town called Holiday Beach. It was postcard pretty. A scenic lake, lots of trees, and some rocky hills to break up the horizon. There didn't seem to be much to it, but I heard the locals talking about some amazing cross-country trails. It also has a terrific restaurant called The Atlas that has the best roasted Brussel sprouts with garlic aioli I've ever had in my life."

"I didn't know you were a fan," Jilly said. Not that she and Ben had eaten many meals together, but they'd run into each other at The Pumpkin Patch now and again. A deep and abiding love for Brussel sprouts sounded like something that would have come up.

"I'm not," he replied with a laugh, "but when you show up for lunch at The Atlas on Meatless Monday and have to wait in line for the chance to order the special of a portobello burger with roasted Brussel sprouts as a side, that's what you order. Well, that and apple spice cake with vanilla ice cream."

It didn't sound like a meal which would be her first choice. "I'm sorry you had to suffer through that."

"Me too. So sorry, I did it twice. After I finished eating, I got another burger and side to go and had it for supper while I was waiting to cross the border. Speaking of..." Ben's voice trailed off as he held up his finger in the "one minute" sign and walked to his coat. He pulled a thick envelope from an interior pocket and returned to the table. "Invoices, receipts, and other assorted paperwork from this last trip. It's all there."

"I'll get it to the warehouse first thing," she promised. This close to Christmas, the contents of Ben's trailer would be unloaded, sorted, and back on the road by the end of the day tomorrow. "Will you miss long haul driving?"

A frown flickered over Ben's face. He shrugged. "I loved it when I started, but after twenty years, a lot of the shine has worn off. I enjoy seeing new places like Holiday Beach, but I won't be sorry to get off the road. I can discover new places when I'm on vacation," he said.

"Do you think you'll like working in a cubicle, after all that freedom?" As executive assistant to the vice-president of Human Resources, she liked to make sure the people they hired were happy. Unhappy employees tended to move on quickly, and Jilly wanted to keep Ben in town as long as she could.

With the hot chocolate drunk and the paperwork handed over, Ben pulled on his coat. "I guess we're about to find out."

CHAPTER 2

BEN FREDERICKS GRINNED as he looked around the warehouse. North Pole Unlimited took Christmas seriously, even to the extent of wrapping the huge, rolling dock doors in lights. Unlike in the corporate offices, nobody here wore Santa hats because they were a safety violation, but carols played over the loudspeakers and talk of presents and the town parade dominated the conversations.

Jilly, as she always did because she was amazing, had dropped off his trip sheets and invoices at the warehouse offices when she got to work that morning, which allowed them to start unloading while he got to sleep in after a four-day trip. Eight hours in his own bed, followed by a shower that drained the hot water tank had him feeling human again.

Now he was ready for more paperwork. Life-changing paperwork.

He was surprised to find Nick Klassen, the vice president of Human Resources, waiting for him outside the warehouse manager's office. "So this is it? Are you sure you want to hang up your trucker's hat?" Nick asked.

"My big rig days are about to be officially behind me."

"Then let's start you on your new career."

Ben and Nick walked through the parking lots separating the distribution centre from the administrative buildings and the manufacturing warehouses. Waist-high snowbanks covered what would be beds overflowing with flowers in the summer. Ben didn't often get to wander through the whole North Pole Unlimited complex, and he was shocked all over again at how big it was.

Nick guided him through the administrative wing, pointed out the Logistics division where he'd be working, the I.T. department, and most importantly, Nick stressed, the company cafeteria. When they finally arrived at Nick's offices, Ben paused in the hall. He hoped everything was going to go along with his grand plan.

Jilly didn't look up from her computer screen when they entered. "Heads up, boss. I threatened to beat Dr. Kovac with a pool noodle if she doesn't submit her third quarter personnel review sheets by the end of the week. I don't care how many Ph.D.'s Tinka has. I'll take her down if I have to send her a fourth reminder."

"I'll call her personally," Nick said, and Ben stifled a grin at the six foot three Viking giving Jilly's desk an extra-wide berth.

"You don't mess around when it comes to deadlines," Ben said in greeting.

That got her attention. Jilly's fingers paused above the keyboard as she froze for a second. "Hi there!"

"Hi."

"Hi," she said again. "Was there a problem at the warehouse? I gave them everything you gave me last night. Did something fall out of your envelope?" She pulled her purse from under her desk and began rummaging through it.

"No, everything was fine."

Nick grinned at the two of them. "Jilly Lewis, I'd like to introduce Ebenezer Fredericks, our newest hire."

She tilted her head to stare at her boss. "Really, Nick?"

Nick barreled on as if she hadn't spoken. "Mr. Fredericks is the new logistics trainee. He'll be starting with Kristen Gillam to learn the ropes for transport coordination before he gets assigned a region. Mr. Fredericks, this is Jilly Lewis, the second-best administrative assistant working at North Pole Unlimited," Nick continued.

"Second best?" Jilly asked with mock concern.

"Ginger Malone, Gabriel Conner's second in command over in the Toy division, shares her Christmas cookies with me," Nick said.

"Second best is good enough for you, boss."

Ben laughed. He knew how lucky he was. Jilly's Scrooge-like tendency when it came to sharing cookies was legendary.

"In that case, welcome to the new team, *Ebenezer*," she said. "I'd give you the usual warnings, but I already know you're good with paperwork and reports, so I won't have to pull out my pool noodle. But in case you get any ideas about slacking off..." Jilly opened her lower desk drawer and drew out a foam tube the length of her forearm.

Ben lost it and howled in laughter. So did Nick. "You promised me you'd get rid of that thing!" Nick said.

"Some people need the reminder. Like for, oh, getting

me the paperwork for new hires more than ten minutes before they show up for work," she hinted.

"Come into my office, Ben. Let's get those forms signed before Jilly turns on us."

"You are so well-trained, boss," was Jilly's unconcerned retort as her attention returned to her computer.

Nick's office matched his energetic personality, with a treadmill in the corner and multiple televisions along one wall. The only thing out of place was the stuffed bass wearing a mini-Santa hat mounted above the window. It came alive when Nick took his seat behind his desk. The fish started flapping and singing the chorus to "Sweet Caroline."

"That is deeply disturbing," Ben said.

"I know."

"Can't you turn it off?"

"No. I can't reach the switch. Believe me, I've been trying for four years. It's bolted to a beam somehow. Jilly said she had Maintenance look at it, and it can't come off without taking down part of the wall. I'll have to wait till the next round of renovations." Nick glared at the fish.

"How has that thing not run out of batteries in the last four years?" Ben asked.

Nick's blue eyes went wide. "I'm going to kill her."

Ben wanted to laugh at the fact Jilly had kept a prank running for four years. It was going to be so much fun working here. "Maybe you could hold off on that until January. I'm glad to see her showing some Christmas spirit." He took the offered pen and began signing at all the flagged locations.

"You're glad to see Jilly showing some Christmas spirit? Have you not met my assistant before? Her picture is in the dictionary."

"Not this year, it isn't. Did you notice she has nothing up at her desk?" Ben had. Every other office he'd passed had been decked out with Christmas decorations, a celebration of lights for Hanukkah or Kwanzaa, or countdowns to the new year, be it calendar, Chinese or Ukrainian. Jilly, on the other hand, had stacks of files, a small crystal candy bowl filled with an assortment of wrapped nougats and chocolate kisses, and a book with yarn on the cover balancing precariously on the corner of her desk. There wasn't a candy cane or stocking in sight.

Nick frowned when he handed over another stack of forms. He went to his door, opened it, looked into the outer office, then closed it again. "What's wrong with her? Is she sick?"

"She's boycotting Christmas," Ben said.

"What? Why?"

"She told me none of her family will be around on the twenty-fifth, so she doesn't feel like there's any reason for her to celebrate."

"But Christmas is her thing," Nick protested. "She must have been joking."

Ben leaned forward, trying to emphasize the importance of the news he was about to share. "She took the leaves out of her dining room table, and she doesn't have a single decoration up at home. I think she's serious."

"That can't be. She must need a holiday jump-start." Nick nodded to himself. "I'll take care of it. It's disappointing to hear about her family, but I'm sure she'll come around. In the meantime, let's introduce you to your new department and make sure they're ready for you."

Nick walked him to the door. "Jilly, will you take Ben over to Logistics so he can talk to Kristen about his training schedule? Here's his file. If we missed anything, please grab him before the end of the day so he's ready to go first thing tomorrow."

She set the file on top of her keyboard and grabbed her security pass. "Let's acquaint you with your new desk."

The walk back to the Logistics division took much longer than it had the first time, probably because people were willing to flag them down to talk to Jilly and ask her questions, whereas everyone had been much too busy to look up when Nick walked by.

Jilly kept up a running commentary as she introduced him to his coworkers in his new department, from how long they'd worked at North Pole Unlimited, to their educational backgrounds, to whether or not they participated in any of the company's sport leagues. She talked to and about everybody.

But the number one topic people wanted to discuss with her was Christmas. Did Jilly have a list of floats for the parade? Did she know Madison Hill was selling wrapping paper for a school fundraiser and her father Tim had the order sheet? Had she signed up for the office bake exchange that Ginger Malone was organizing?

"How do you expect to escape Christmas working in a place like this?" Ben asked. It was everywhere. He was surprised she'd held out this long. "It's the beginning of December. It's only going to get worse."

Jilly crossed her arms. "I'll find a way."

He was in for a fight and was looking forward to every minute of it.

CHAPTER 3

AVOIDING the holidays would be harder than she thought. Signs—figurative and literal—were everywhere, and they were insidious. Being known as the Christmas Queen around the office had seemed like a good idea when she started at North Pole Unlimited years ago, but now, when people were stopping by her desk for just that reason, Jilly was reconsidering her title. The constant cheer rubbed her the wrong way, but she'd invited it upon herself, so she couldn't complain too much.

Jilly found a real smile when little Madison Hill ran into her office and gave her a hug as a thank you for the birthday wrapping paper order she'd placed. Jilly could be as miserable as she wanted, but she wasn't going to poison anyone else's holiday spirit.

She might have to do something creative to her boss, though. Once she was back from lunch after dealing with Ben's surprise paperwork, Nick called her into his office.

The bass above his desk greeted her.

"Once we get that thing unbolted from the wall, I

have to check to see what kind of batteries it runs on," Nick said as he pulled a file from his drawer.

"I'm sure you'll be surprised." She was pleased her voice held steady for her answer. It hadn't been easy switching them out every six months without getting caught.

"But until then, I have an urgent staffing problem I need you to solve." He slapped a thick manila folder, bulging with paper and paperclips holding various photos to papers, onto his desk. "Enjoy, and good luck." He didn't look at her when she flipped through it.

"This is for a float in the December Christmas parade."

"Yes, it is."

"This isn't one of my projects."

"It is now."

"No, the Santa Claus float is sponsored by the Klassen family personally. I took care of the company entry already," Jilly protested.

Organizing the parade float had been fun. Of course, she still thought she'd been celebrating Christmas when she planned the design of the trailer which would be pulled down December's Main Street. The flatbed would be decked out as Santa's workshop, with snowsuit-wearing volunteers dressed as elves tossing candy canes to people cheering from the curb. It wasn't easy coming up with a new theme every year, but Jilly planned each design months in advance. She'd usually have an idea for next year by now.

But it had been a lot of work. Weeks of work. She didn't have time to put together a float in less than a month.

"You don't have to deal with the float itself. I checked

it out already. Santa's Sleigh is in good shape and ready for another year's trip around town," Nick said, saving himself from a pool noodle beating. Then he continued, "The problem is that Mr. and Mrs. Claus are A.W.O.L., and since they're your parents, I'm putting you in charge of finding their replacements."

That wasn't fair. It wasn't her fault her parents were celebrating their anniversary on a different continent. "Are you telling me your grandmother didn't scramble over the dining room table to volunteer when this news came up?" Jilly asked. She'd worked with Adelaide Klassen for over a decade before the company's former president had resigned a couple years earlier. Adelaide may have retired, but she definitely hadn't stopped working. She'd shifted her focus from the business to family and friends. Dressing up as Mrs. Claus to serve the community would be right up her alley.

"Feel free to ask her. Ask everybody. Just please find somebody. You're the Christmas miracle worker. Do your thing. You have two weeks to fill those red velvet sleigh seats," Nick informed her.

She sighed and thought of the coffee cup she used to have that said, *If you want something done, give it to a busy person.* At least this assignment wouldn't take long. All she needed to do was make one call to Adelaide, and she could give Nick the file back.

In theory.

A weak hack sounded on the other end of the line. "I can't. I've come down with a mild chest cold that I can't shake." A faint sneeze. "At my age, I can't be too careful."

"Adelaide, you have the constitution of an ox. You'll be fine." Jilly knew Adelaide was on two curling teams and two community boards. She had a more active social life than Jilly did. She was never down for long.

"Sorry, dear. You'll have to find someone else to be Mrs. Claus. Or don the red cloak yourself."

That wasn't happening. Ever. "I'll make some calls. Feel better, Adelaide."

Jilly steepled her fingers. She had no Plan B. Mrs. Claus's rosy cheeks could be achieved with rouge, and Mr. Claus's bowl-full-of-jelly belly was only a pillow away, but who did she know who'd be willing to play dress-up?

Jilly didn't have the time or energy for this. Not between the year-end paperwork and the constant interruptions. She needed help, someone who'd done this before. She needed... "Rudy Gillespie, my favourite warehouse manager in all of the Prairies, how are you?" she asked, after a frantic hunt for an out-of-province phone number.

"Uh, oh. What do you want, Jilly?" was the cautious reply.

"Nothing bad. A simple referral," she said. Rudy had been in this exact same position a year ago and pulled a Santa out of his hat at the last minute for his community Christmas party. He'd have a list of suggestions for her. "I need a man in a red suit."

Hysterical laughter made her pull the receiver away from her ear. "This month? Good luck with that," Rudy said unhelpfully.

"You did it. Surely you have a list."

"First of all, stop calling me Shirley. Second, yes, I've got a list. I used it *last* December, the day after the party that almost wasn't, to book my guest of honour for *this* year. You won't find anybody available last minute."

"I know you have contacts. There's got to be some-body. What if I sweeten the pot with a dozen imported chocolate meringues?" It was the best bribe in her arsenal.

The laughter got louder.

"Two dozen." She could afford to take that out of her personal holiday cookie stash. Barely. It would be a sacri-fice, but a necessary one to get this task off her to-do list.

"Imported? Nice try, Jilly, but I'm dating the baker that makes those for you, remember?"

Shoot. She'd forgotten that Rudy was seeing Kris Singleton, who was also in Calgary. The Totally Iced baker had sent her a private order of her favourite cookies back in November. They were excellent incentives in the office, but apparently, they weren't going to work in this situation. "What kind of bribe would work?"

Rudy's voice lost its amusement. "If you're serious, I'm sorry, but I don't think I can help. I have no idea where our Santa came from last year. Honestly, until this conversation, I was still convinced you had sent him to help us out and were denying it as a joke. Give me a minute." She heard paper shuffling on the other end of the line. "I'll send you an email of all my leads. You may be able to find similar companies or services in your area. Frankly, at this point, you may have to do what I did."

"What was that?"

"Rent a suit," Rudy said. "I was already dressed when our mysterious man in red appeared. I hid in a storeroom till he left, then changed back to my regular clothes."

"We already have the costumes, Rudy."

"Then what's the problem? Practice your ho-ho-ho's and fill those shiny black boots yourself."

"Not on your life."

"I don't know what else to tell you, Jilly. I'll send you the list, but you're on your own."

"I'm telling Kris to ban you from the bakery."

He laughed again. "I'm her number one quality control supervisor. It'll never stick. Good luck, Jilly. And Merry Christmas."

Rudy was as good as his word. An email appeared in her in box a couple minutes later, listing various talent agencies and actors-for-hire. He'd also added a list of search terms to use online and a reminder that they'd probably be booked.

She couldn't believe her parents had left her in this predicament.

Double humbug.

CHAPTER 4

HE WAS GOING to like it here. His trainer was knowledgeable, the other people in the logistics division had welcomed him with open arms, and he had the option to use a headset or not when talking on the phone. Ben was a definite "not," but it was nice to have the choice.

He was also gratified to learn that his long-haul career had lasting value. Policy was well and good, but things happened on the road that could not be predicted or avoided. His practical knowledge meant the entire office would have the benefit of his experiences.

All that was left to do was return some final paperwork to Human Resources, and then he'd be done for the day, with his first day of actual work to start at eight o'clock the next morning. As he retraced his steps to Jilly's desk, he ran into Joy McCall-Harkness in the corridor.

Ben didn't know the auburn-haired employee well, but he knew she worked as a veterinary assistant, even without the clues of two leashes hanging out of her jacket pockets and a feather stuck to her shoulder. Ben held a fire door open for her, since both her hands were full of shopping bags. "Where are you headed?" he asked.

"I need to see Jilly before I return to my litter of Tasmanian kittens," she said.

"Is that a breed? I haven't heard of them before."

Joy laughed. "No. I call them that because they are all little devils. Devils with escape artist genes. I'm pretty sure some of the older cats have been giving them lessons on how to open their cage doors. I'll miss them when they're gone, but right now, I'd like to, just once, find them where I left them," she complained.

Ben caught a peek inside one of Joy's bags. "Is that whole bag full of toques?"

"You bet." She raised the one in her left hand. "Hats." Then her right hand. "Slippers."

"You're a knitting machine!"

"This wasn't all me. These are donations from the Southern Manitoba Fibre Association. They make them all year for distribution to various charities during the holidays. I'm part of the wrapping committee. Which is why I need to speak to Jilly."

Ben had no problem waiting while the two women discussed yarn business. He was simply thrilled to have experienced a normal office workday. He started paying attention when Joy picked up the bags she'd set on the floor.

"I can do that," Jilly said to Joy. "I'll grab the list from the Sunset tonight and get it to you tomorrow."

"Thank you. The sooner I can scratch the wrapping job off my ever-growing to-do list, the happier I'll be," Joy said.

"Did you get the wrapping paper from Tim Hill?"

"No, one of Madison's classmates' parents works in Veterinary Services. He got my business this year."

"It's all for a good cause. Have a good night."

Jilly was pleasant but professional when he handed over his paperwork. It took her ten minutes to go through each form to make sure every "I" was dotted and every "T" crossed. He thought he'd done a good job, but one signature and three initials later gave him new appreciation for her thoroughness, especially since his future paycheques were on the line. When she was done, she locked the file in a drawer and turned off her computer screen.

"Are you done for the day?" he asked.

"Yes. I'll get that done tomorrow, but I'll backdate it to today," Jilly promised.

"I wasn't worried about that. Did I hear you say you were heading to the Sunset? The Sunset Retirement Residence?"

"Yes."

"Me too. Want a ride?"

"Thank you, but I've got my car."

"I can walk you to your car and help with the bags," he offered.

"That I'll say thanks to." Jilly pulled her navy ski jacket from the coat rack by the door. The bright pink scarf she wrapped around her neck contrasted with the coat and reminded him of an Easter egg. "Why are you going to the Sunset?" she asked.

"I'm visiting my mom. She moved into the supported living side this past fall, and I'm not handling it well, so I want to check on her." His mother had been one of his reasons for getting off the road. He was fifty, and in good shape. His mother was seventy-four and had been on a slow decline for the last five years. Ben had been happy to check in on her every day when he was in town. The problem was that he was often out of town on a run for three or four days at a time. It was especially inconvenient in the winter. His mother couldn't handle shoveling even a light dusting of snow off her front walk. She agreed to let him hire a housekeeper for her, but the past spring, she told him she'd had enough.

"*I've been on my own for six years since your father passed, rambling around this house on my own. I think it's time I downsized and had someone on hand regularly in case I need help,*" she'd told him over a simple supper he'd prepared while tulips bloomed outside the kitchen window.

"*Would you like live-in help? I think we could arrange that.*"

"*No, I want to sell the house and move into a retirement community.*"

He still remembered the shock he felt, like he'd let her down by not helping her enough. "*But, Mom, you don't need that kind of care. I can do more around the house. We can also get someone to come every day.*"

"*Sweetie, this isn't about you. I'm old, and my bones are telling me so. Getting rid of the house and all the responsibilities that come with it is a choice at this point, and I want to be in charge of my future. If I sell now, while I'm still relatively healthy, I can choose the next place I move into, rather than rattling around here and getting moved straight into a care home with nothing in between. Don't you think assisted living would be a good middle step for me right now?*"

No, he'd thought it was a horrible step. One that she probably wouldn't have considered if he'd been home more regularly. Ben had quickly run through all the options he could think of, from hiring a daily homecare worker, to moving back in to keep an eye on his mother. But eventually he had to admit that unless he could come up with a solution they both liked, it was up to her.

A suite had opened at the Sunset Retirement Residence just before Hallowe'en, and she had moved in at the beginning of November. He still hated visiting her there when he thought of how much happier she would be in her own house.

"Parents can be tough," Jilly agreed. She pulled on pink mittens that matched her scarf and handed him both bags of knitting. He almost said something until he saw her pull two more bags from under her desk.

She grinned at his look. "We have a lot of donations. There are quite a few seniors at the Sunset living on their own who don't have anyone to celebrate the holidays with. Flora Mercado has a list of residents and locals without families who come to their community events. She asks them what they'd like for Christmas, and most of the things are really simple. Slippers, hand lotion, large print puzzle books. Making sure they have something to unwrap on Christmas morning is a little thing. My knitting group makes sure everybody gets a handmade present."

"What happened to your anti-holiday stance?"

"That's for me. I'm won't keep other people from celebrating." Her grin wavered. "Come on. Help me carry."

"Will you have to wrap and deliver all these yourself?" Ben asked. She'd be running around for days.

Perhaps she needed some help of the professional-driver variety.

"No, I'm collection central. We have a committee. Joy's the leader."

Ben nodded. "Let me know if I can help." That would be a good way to get involved in the community and an excuse to socialize. Joy would know who he could talk to so he could best lend a hand. She didn't know it yet, but Jilly was about to get a new helper.

"I will, thanks. I just need this day to end."

A brisk, cold wind buffeted them as they walked to their cars. The sun was already low in the sky, which meant it would be full dark by the time they got home. It was the worst thing about the season. "What else went wrong? Did my surprise paperwork throw you off schedule that badly?" he asked.

Jilly's head came up sharply. "No, not at all. Nick dropped another project in my lap this morning right after you came into the office. I need to find a Santa and Mrs. Claus for the town float in the December parade, and I can't find any volunteers. All the people I thought would jump at the chance have turned me down flat."

"Why don't you do it?" He threw up his hands before she had a chance to object. "If you were celebrating Christmas this year, would you do it?"

"Not a chance. I'm not a put on a costume and appear in public person. I prefer to work behind the scenes."

"I can respect that." He wasn't a costume person either. When it came to Hallowe'en, he put on a ball cap and a hockey jersey and said he was dressed as a sports fan. He found it endearing that Jilly's decoration-mania was focused on one calendar holiday and not all of them. "Can I help?"

"Do you want to be Santa?"

"As much as you want to be Mrs. Claus," he said quickly. He was not accidentally volunteering for float duty. Even if his mom would get a kick out of it.

"Then no. I'm stuck." She gave a small smile. "Unless I find another sucker. I mean volunteer."

CHAPTER 5

THE SUNSET RETIREMENT RESIDENCE was not as overwhelmingly decorated as Jilly had feared. They had a lovely red-and-silver tree in the corner, with a red tree skirt and some wrapped presents beneath it. Twin poinsettias sat at either end of the reception counter. The rest of the lobby was kept clear for wheelchairs and walkers. "Good evening, Ms. Lewis," the tiny, black-haired woman behind the counter said in greeting. "Hi, Mr. Fredericks. Your mother's playing bingo in the common room right now."

"Thanks, Flora." Ben gave her a wave before he headed to the elevator.

"Great timing, Ms. Lewis. I'm finishing my shift. Why don't you come into my office?" Flora Mercado said.

The social director's desk was clear, but the cabinets behind her were piled high with paper and books and brochures. She studied the chaos carefully and slid a blue folder from a stack. "I have your list. My guests are already looking forward to it. Thanks again for doing this."

"It's no problem at all. It's nice to make things for people who will appreciate them." All the members of the Southern Manitoba Fibre Association were serious yarn collectors. They would never use all their wool, so donating a crocheted or knitted project or two gave them a chance to use a skein which would otherwise never see the light of day. Jilly herself preferred to knit slippers. Joy was a hatmaker. Dr. Tinka Kovac in Research and Development whipped up a new pair of socks every two weeks.

"All your gifts are greatly appreciated. I don't have to tell you some of long-term guests have put in special requests. I hope someone was able to make Mrs. Johnson her annual Blue Bombers toque in the proper shades of blue and gold."

"It's in my trunk," Jilly promised. After six years, the locally famous colour combination was the first thing she looked for. "What other things are on the wish list?"

Flora handed her the folder. Jilly took a breath before she opened it. The handmade donations were easy, and if they needed more, the group could whip off some more in a week. The rest could be a challenge. They had a limited budget to purchase things, so she hoped they had enough to cover everything. A quick scan didn't reveal anything outrageous, but the sheer number left her with a bottom line that made her gasp.

"Yes, we've had a few more additions this year," Flora said. "Will it be okay?"

"We'll make it work." Jilly could kick in a little more, and there were plenty of people at the office who would donate. Ben probably would too, especially with his mom being a new resident. "I'll take this with me and get shopping. We're having our first wrapping party this weekend, so please let me know if anything changes before Christmas."

"I will. Thanks again."

Jilly left feeling a little less grumpy about the upcoming work. If she could talk one of the other committee members into purchasing the Scotch tape and other accessories, she wouldn't have to dig out her own bin of tissue paper and bows and ribbons, which would give her a jumpstart on getting her house back to normal. She knew she needed to put away the decorations, but she couldn't work up the desire to do that. She was in a weird Christmas limbo, not wanting to celebrate it but feeling guilty after Dan went to the trouble of trying to make up for the fact he'd be away. He'd even given her a brand-new wreath for the front door that was still in the box.

She looked twice when she saw Ben in the lobby as she was leaving. "I thought you were visiting your mom."

"Apparently she's on a roll in bingo. She's won the last two games, and only has five numbers to go for a blackout. I'm a distraction, so she sent me home. I'll try again tomorrow."

"I don't know if I should say sorry or be glad she's settling in." She also made a note to add bingo daubers to her shopping list.

"Be glad."

"Okay." He looked a little less stressed than when they'd arrived, but he still had tight lines around his eyes. "Was something else wrong?"

"No. I had an idea, but I don't want to annoy you."

"How could you annoy me?"

"It's about Christmas. In particular, your float problem."

"I won't be annoyed if you came up with a solution."

In fact, she'd be willing to give him a dozen chocolate meringues if that would get the file off her desk.

"Okay, here it is. This entire place is covered in Christmas decorations. It is full of seniors, a lot of them without family, who are desperately trying to find a way to take part in the holidays. Why don't you ask the residents if they want to be the parade's headliners? I bet you'll get volunteers."

Jilly closed her mouth and thought about it for a minute. Obviously, the residents receiving full-time care couldn't be on a float, outside, for two hours in the dead of winter. But what about the ones who were already on various volunteer projects around December, the ones like Adelaide who had more active social lives than she did? Ben might have solved her Santa setback.

She grabbed him by the hand, turned on her heel, and marched back into Flora's office. The other woman was pulling her scarf out of her coat sleeve. "I need a Mr. and Mrs. Claus for December's Christmas parade. Do you think anyone here would be interested in donning the big red suit for a good cause?" Jilly asked.

Flora paused, her arm awkwardly behind her head with her scarf hanging over her ear. "I think I can find a person or two who might be interested. I'll let you know."

"Terrific." Another problem solved. "Thank you."

Jilly pulled Ben back into the hall. "And thank you too. Do you want to come over tonight for appreciation cookies and cocoa?"

He made a face. "Can I have a rain check? I've been waiting for this day since I applied for my new job. I have a date with another lady tonight." He paused, then gave her a sly smile. "Would you like to come along to meet her?"

CHAPTER 6

IT WAS A RISK. Jilly should know his sense of humour by now, but Ben knew she was a little off her stride. Fortunately, she smiled and took the bait. "I'd love to be your third wheel. I'm sure it won't be awkward at all."

"I'll pick you up at quarter to seven."

He still needed to do a full grocery shop now that he was home for good, but Ben made do with tomato soup and a grilled cheese sandwich for supper. His mother had invited him to eat with her in the dining room. To show him they didn't just feed her gruel, and that the meals were both tasty and healthy, she'd said, but he declined.

"Maybe next time," he'd told her. "I have a hot date in a couple hours."

"Oh, that's tonight. Get out of here!"

His mother had been eagerly waiting for an introduction to the new woman in his life. Ben couldn't wait for them to meet either. His preparations for his big night didn't take long. First, he got changed. He needed stuff that could get soiled if he got down and rolled around in the dirt, but nothing too ragged, since he still had to make a good impression. A black T-shirt, a plaid flannel shirt, and thick jeans would serve him well for what was to come.

He hoped Jilly like who he was bringing home for the night. He'd already committed to the relationship, so it would be awkward if they didn't get along.

Jilly raced out of her house and jumped into his car before he had a chance to think about getting out. "Crank the heat," she said. "It's getting colder by the minute." She looked at the blanket-covered box in the back seat but didn't say a word about it. "Where are we going?"

"Out to the Graham place. I'm picking up a blonde to take home with me."

Jilly hooted in delight. "Awesome! Give me details."

Ben pulled his phone out of his pocket and quickly called up a series of photos. "Isn't she a pretty girl?" A fuzzy golden puppy smiled on the screen. Subsequent pictures had her sitting, sleeping, and in a pile of similar puppies curled against their mother. "She's twelve weeks old today. Penny kept her an extra month until I was finished on the road. I finally get to bring her home."

"She's adorable."

"I checked with the regulations at the Sunset. They allow four-legged visitors, so I can bring her along when I visit my mom, once she's fully trained." His mom had a dog companion for years, but when her last one had passed away, she insisted she didn't have the energy for a new puppy. Looking back, he could see it had been a sign of what was to come.

This was much better. Now, when he saw her, she'd have all the fun and none of the training or clean up. Besides, he wanted a warm body to greet him when he came in the door after work. Too many years of time alone in his rig and in motels had left him sensitive to empty rooms.

"What's her name?"

"Sprite."

"That's perfect. She looks like a Sprite."

She did. She had big, light brown eyes and long eyelashes. The big feet at the end of her stubby legs promised she'd grow out of the fluffball stage into a medium sized dog. The shape of her eyes and mouth gave her the impression of a happy, smiling dog, like a golden retriever, although kennel owner Penny Graham had warned him that she was no purebred. She was half golden retriever, half sneaky neighbour's dog. It was why the owner gave them up and Penny had a litter to give away.

"Thanks for coming. I think I'll need an extra pair of hands tonight," he said.

"Let's go. I'm happy to be a third wheel on your date with Sprite."

He already had the dog food bowls, the treats, the training pads, the kennel, and the booties and sweaters for walks at home. He'd started planning as soon as he heard the puppies would be available. Now all he had to do was get the dog.

The midnight blue sky was full of stars as they drove out of December into the darkness. The clear sky meant a cold night, but they weren't outside long. Penny Graham was waiting at the kennel's front doors. "Come in, come in. We're finishing our evening playtime." They stepped into a huge room that ran the length of the converted barn. One side was fenced off, giving the dogs a twenty-five metre sprint track. Two employees were chasing a pack of various breeds around the room. Ben couldn't tell who was more tired, the workers or the dogs with their tongues hanging out of their mouths.

"Your girl is waiting for you. Thanks for bringing in your old sweatshirt. She's been sleeping with it all week. Are you ready to meet her?"

"I'm ready."

Penny waved at a woman waiting by the entrance to the kennel room. She opened the door, and a little blonde fuzzball stumbled into the room, tripping over its feet.

"Oh, I'm in love," Jilly whispered, as the puppy crouched over Ben's boots, its little butt wiggling in excitement.

"Hello, sweetheart." Ben lowered his hand. Sprite sniffled it, then gave it a lick.

It took Sprite some time to calm down enough to be taken to the cage waiting in the back seat. Once she was settled, he and Jilly jumped into the warm car. "Are you a dog person?" he asked.

"Generally, I'm a cat person, but for that sweetie, I'd make an exception."

A cat person. He didn't know that about her. He'd seen a few cat toys around her house when he first dropped by, but hadn't seen a sign of anything kitty-related since then.

"Would you like to come up and help me get her settled?"

"Nah, I've horned in enough for one night. You two need to get used to each other. But I expect another invitation soon. And pictures daily."

Ben admitted to himself Jilly was right. He needed bonding time with Sprite. He swung back down Jilly's street and pulled into her driveway. "Thanks for coming out with me tonight."

"Thank you. This was a treat. Thank you for not making it about Christmas. I was worried you might push. I appreciate that you didn't."

His face must have betrayed him, because when she looked at him, she laughed. "You might have thought about it, but you restrained yourself."

"I was distracted. I still plan to convince you to give this season another try."

"Give it your best shot," she said as she got out of the car.

He waved when she turned on her front step once she had the door open. Then he turned to face the back seat. "Did you hear that, Sprite? She said I could give it my best shot." He rubbed his hands together. "Let's get home and start planning."

CHAPTER 7

EVERY YEAR, she managed to forget how crazy work got in December. Jilly stayed in the office till six o'clock, hoping for some quiet time to catch up on scheduling, but everyone else had the same idea, and she barely made a dent in her to-do pile before she quit for the night. Now, after changing into leggings and heating a frozen pasta meal in the microwave, she snuggled into the corner of her sofa with a glass of wine within reach, wondering who would be sent home that week on her favourite reality show.

As she thought about all the people she'd sent out of her office during the week, Ben's name was conspicuously absent. He hadn't disappeared entirely. They'd waved to each other across the cafeteria. She'd run into him at the Sunset Retirement Residence and said hello in passing as he headed off to see his mother while she got an updated gift recipient list from Flora. She was used to him coming over for a visit once or twice a week when he got back from his runs, but that had stopped. She missed him.

She didn't miss Sprite, though. Ben was diligent about

sending her daily photos. He made dogs look so cute she was almost reconsidering her cat preference.

Movement caught her attention out of the corner of her eye. A familiar puppy was pulling a bundled-up human down the sidewalk. When the dog paused to take interest in the snowbank, the human looked up and waved. When he pointed at her, Jilly nodded and jumped to her feet.

She wrapped the throw blanket from the sofa around her shoulders and opened the front door. Her porchlight flickered once and then went dark with an audible *pop*. Rather than stand in the dark, Jilly growled and fished at an extension cord that was wrapped around the front steps railing. When she plugged it into the electrical outlet below the light, the front of her house burst into red and green stars as the lights around the door and window sprang to life. "A little far from home, aren't you?"

Ben laughed. "My dog is defective. Sprite doesn't have an off button. She can walk for hours. I've already put on enough miles to make up for one year of being on the road."

"It's been four days."

He gave her a pained look. "I know. But she's a puppy —what am I going to do?"

"Invest in new boots, apparently." Jilly watched as Sprite strained at the leash. "I should let you continue in your efforts to wear her out."

"Thanks. Another ten blocks should do it for tonight. Then she'll sleep all night until she wakes me up at six to do it again."

She ought to buy Ben new sneakers for Christmas. New shoelaces at the very least. "Have a good time. Good night."

"Wait!"

She froze with her hand on the door.

"Would you, and feel free to say no, but would you like to go out to dinner with me?" Ben asked her. Clouds of steam erupted from his mouth as he waited for her response.

It had been a while since she'd been on a real date. The last time she'd gone out with someone, it had ended badly after he'd met her son. This time, though, she'd be on a date with someone who was already a friend. Although that came with its own risks, she thought Ben would be worth it. "Okay."

His huge smile at her response told her she'd made the right decision. "Tomorrow? I can get a babysitter for Sprite."

It was the only night she had off this week. "That sounds great."

"Terrific. I'll pick you up at six."

She was thankful work the next day was so busy that she didn't have time to obsess over all the details she didn't get from him. Where were they going? How should she dress?

She went with a thick black sweater and black wool pants. A chunky silver necklace and matching earrings she'd picked up in Texas added some sparkle.

Ben looked good too. She was glad she hadn't gone business formal. He looked great in his dress shirt and tie, and he'd added a sports coat she'd never seen before. Jilly's heart skipped a beat when he walked toward her.

"Where are we eating?"

"The Prairie Grill," Ben said. "I hope you don't mind." Jilly had heard of the restaurant but had never gone there herself. It specialized in locally sourced food.

In a short time, the restaurant had developed a huge following for their fresh fish from the nearby lakes and their fresh breads made from Manitoba grains. With local farmers selling their last vegetable pickings for the season, it was a perfect time to try it.

It was a short drive south of December, putting it about an hour outside of Winnipeg. Even at that distance, though, there was a line at the door. "This place is hopping," Ben said.

Although Ben had made reservations, it took some time for them to be seated. Their table was along a wall of windows. The Red River outside was a flowing stream of shining black and silver moonlight. The sun was long gone, but the rising moon lit the clear sky. The menu was small but full of dishes. They ordered—freshly made spaghetti and marinara sauce with mushrooms for her, and pickerel over wild rice with carrots for him.

"This is amazing. How often do you eat here?" Jilly asked.

"I drove by it for eight months before I had a chance to come. The first time, I brought my mom for her birthday. It was nice, and the food was great. This is my second time."

"I'm glad she liked it. I'll have to recommend it to my parents when they get back."

"Where are they?"

"They left yesterday for Sydney. They should have landed by now. Then they have a bunch of tours lined up for the next three weeks. The Outback. The Gold Coast."

"Sounds like fun."

"It does. I wish they could have waited till after Christmas. I think they would have liked it more then. You don't need a break from winter in December. They should have gone in late January instead." Jilly needed to get over being abandoned for the holidays, so she tried to change the topic. "Originally, they had a cruise planned, but they changed their minds. Have you ever been on a cruise?"

"Yes. It was an unforgettable experience."

"So you liked it?" She'd never been on one herself, but everyone she knew who'd taken one seemed to have enjoyed it.

"No. I had no idea I was susceptible to severe sea sickness. I swear the ground was still rocking a week later. It was horrible."

"Oh, no!" But she still laughed at his queasy expression.

"I prefer to hit places with hiking and biking trails. Provincial parks. Summer resort towns. How about you?" Ben asked.

"I prefer land-based holidays. Chicago, Atlanta, Texas, Florida."

His brow wrinkled. "I don't see the connection. It can't be all warm destinations with Chicago in there."

"They're all rollercoaster meccas. Huge parks full of thrills and delight. Daniel and I love them." There was nothing she loved more than the rush of wind in her face and the screams of other terrified riders.

He shook his head. "No way. Rollercoasters are just big boats in the sky. Up, down, left right." He frowned at her. "No thank you."

"I'm sure we'd find some middle ground if we went on vacation together," she said.

The happy spell was interrupted by the waiter. Not any waiter: one bearing a dessert tray, which in normal times would not have been a problem. "For dessert, I recommend any of our seasonal desserts. We have warm gingerbread cake with caramel sauce, candy cane cheese-cake, hot chocolate torte, and mulled wine spice cake."

Jilly bit her tongue hard. She was in the middle of a lovely date. Everything didn't have to be about Christmas, and they couldn't force her to participate. "I'm stuffed from supper, thank you."

She saw Ben eye the cheesecake, but he declined as well and asked for a coffee. She almost felt guilty. But then he picked up their conversation where they'd left off, asking if she'd booked a summer holiday for next year yet, and her discomfort quickly faded.

Mostly.

CHAPTER 8

"SHE'S GETTING WORSE. She turned down dessert because they were holiday inspired. It doesn't have to be, and probably shouldn't be, Christmas-related, but we need to do something to warm her 'getting colder by the minute' heart," Ben reported with concern. The meal he'd shared with Jilly the previous night had been delicious, but there'd been more than enough room left for dessert. He knew Jilly had a sweet tooth. Her obsession with one specific bakery was known throughout the company and two provinces. She should have jumped at the chance for anything the restaurant had.

There was silence at the other end of the line. "I don't think what I have to offer will help," the woman said. "Especially if she's responding like that to Christmas-like names."

"I'm desperate, Joy."

That was an understatement. After a year of evening coffees and an enjoyable friendship, Ben was hoping Jilly would be open to dating. Now he was in December full-time, but the calendar was working against him. He had to break through Jilly's Christmas-block.

He heard pages flipping on the other end of the line. "I have one option for you, but I can't guarantee she'll like it," Joy Harkness said. Ben didn't believe it. If there was any way to melt a frostbitten heart, it would come from Joy's department.

"Let's give it a try. I'll be there to back you up." He would do anything to banish the grinch who'd bodysnatched a person he cared about.

"Fine. Meet me after work at Jilly's office." Ben set his plotting aside for the rest of the afternoon and got back to work planning new routes and improving ways to track shipments as they came in from across the continent to be redistributed and go back out to end up in stockings and under Christmas trees across the country. He'd thought hauling goods had given him a Christmas spirit rush; it was nothing compared to sending them out like one of Santa's elves, knowing someone's Christmas wish was on its way to being fulfilled.

After he logged out for the day, he went to the Animal Care Department, where Joy was under attack. She could either keep the cage door closed but unlocked with one hand, and try to lure kittens to her with the other, or she had to lock the door and chase after the ones who were out of reach and then try to keep them within reach while she unlocked the door.

"Do you want some help?" Ben offered.

"There are two little fuzzballs hiding under the chair over there," Joy said, pointing with her chin. "The rest are all here with their mommas. Who came up with the bright idea to let them run around every afternoon?" She rolled her eyes. "Right, that was me. No wonder Dr. Farnsworth laughed when I suggested it and then insisted I be in charge."

Ben tracked down two of the escapees and brought them back to the veterinary assistant. "Which of these babies is your accomplice in Operation Jilly?"

She pointed to a grey kitten with white socks dozing in the corner of the cage. "Blitzen is my ace in the hole."

Ben winced. "Blitzen?"

"I warned you. We had two litters delivered two days apart. Ten kittens total. Want to guess the other names?"

"I can guess eight, and Rudolph, but what is the tenth?"

"Olive," she said matter-of-factly.

"Olive?"

Joy smiled, then burst into song. "Olive, the other reindeer, who used to laugh and call him names."

"That's horrible." His Dad-joke sense was offended at the pun.

"That's what happens when you have ten kittens to name after you've had too much cough syrup."

"Fair enough." Ben checked his watch, knowing Jilly would be leaving soon. "Are you ready to give this a shot?"

"The worst she can say is no."

Jilly said worse than that. "No, I don't want to foster a kitten over Christmas, especially one named after a reindeer. What makes you think I'd be interested in something like that over the holidays?" She looked almost angry at being asked.

"Lots of reasons. You're a cat person. You lost Buster a couple years ago and said you might want another cat, and this would be a good test to see if you're ready for a permanent pet. You also told me you'll be home, so you're available. You can't blame Blitzen for his name. That was all me."

"Well, you were wrong. I'm not interested. At all. You'll have to find somebody else."

Joy shrugged, and levelled a hard look at Ben. "That's fine. I was just offering. Have a good night, Jilly." Joy glared at him again on the way out, and Ben knew he had some groveling to do.

"Or you could have gone with a much more polite no thank you. But your way worked too," he said.

Jilly pinched her lips together. "She had no business—"

"Asking a friend if she'd like to babysit a kitten for a few days?" Ben finished.

Her lips pursed, and she squeezed her eyes shut. "I owe her an apology, don't I?"

"It wouldn't hurt." Even worse than watching Jilly beat herself up was knowing how out of character her behavior was. Ben didn't know how to help her. He didn't say anything else; she was hard enough on herself for the both of them.

Besides, she wasn't wrong. Her bitter response had crossed a line, and if he hadn't known she and Joy were good friends, he could see it permanently damaging their relationship. Jilly's anger at the holiday was much greater than he'd originally thought. He'd assumed she needed a hand to get over her new aversion. Now Ben was second-guessing the idea he could help her at all.

He was on his way down the hall when Jilly popped out of her door. "Ben!" she yelled.

"What?"

"Can you come back for a minute?"

She was standing behind her desk, phone to her ear, when he returned to her office. Jilly crooked her finger, so he came in to listen.

"This evening? I suppose..." Her brown eyes went impossibly wide. "How many?" Holding the receiver away from her mouth, she silently pleaded, "Help me?"

Whatever she was hearing sounded surprising but not distressing. Ben nodded. "Sure, we can come over tonight. We'll be there at seven thirty," she said. Jilly hung up the phone, the shocked look still on her face.

"Who was that?" Ben asked when she still hadn't spoken after a full minute.

"Flora. She wanted to talk to me about volunteers for the parade float." Her voice lost its stunned tone and moved toward annoyed.

"Did she get one?"

"No," Jilly snapped.

"I'm confused."

"She put a sign-up list on the bulletin board. They've arranged auditions! For tonight. Couldn't they have given me any warning? What if I already had plans?"

"Did you?"

"That's not the point, Ben. I *could* have. This project is one gigantic pain in the behind," she grumbled. "Auditions?"

He stifled a laugh. "Hey, at least now you have options. What are you going to do?"

"Me? No, we. This was your idea, Ben. You're helping. We've got eight Mrs. Clauses and three Santas to choose from tonight."

It was less funny now. "I have to be home with Sprite. I can't leave her alone again so soon."

"You could bring her. I'm sure they'd love to see her. Seven thirty, Ben. Don't make me break out the pool noodle."

CHAPTER 9

SHE WASN'T OVERREACTING. Why would Joy
assume she wanted a cat? Had she told anyone she
wanted a cat? No, she had not. Nobody wanted to have a
bunch of extra responsibilities dumped on them. Especially over Christmas. Jilly had gone through litter box
training before, and it was not a job for the weak of
stomach or those who needed a solid night's sleep. It
required time, patience, and a commitment she hadn't in
any way indicated she wanted.

She wasn't the unreasonable one.

She probably could have used softer language though,
Jilly reluctantly admitted to herself as she emptied the
spaghetti sauce jar into the pan. Joy was just doing her
job, trying to take care of her charges and find them good
homes.

But Jilly wasn't certain she was ready for a new cat.
She definitely didn't want one named Blitzen. Blitzen! It
was asking for trouble. A Blitzen sounded like a kitten
who would be sneaky, fast, and agile. Not to mention a
Blitzen would leave a trail of tumbling vases and knocked

over glasses in its wake. A walking disaster covered in fur. If she were to get a cat, and Jilly didn't say she was, she'd probably go for a senior cat named Fluffy or Bumble who spent her days on a cushion in the sunshine, napping a lot and only moving to come for cuddles or food. That was her speed of cat.

She left the parmesan cheese in the fridge and slapped her bowl of spaghetti and sauce on the table. Now she was stuck auditioning parade float personnel. On her night off. That wasn't in her job description! At least, not for this float. Nick could assign her as many Christmas jobs as he wanted, but he couldn't force her to be jolly when she did them. She couldn't fault residents at the Sunset for applying to an open audition, but she could have a word with Flora for setting it up in the first place.

And her tomato sauce had too much salt.

The only thing that snapped her out of her spiral of grumpiness was the number that appeared on her cell phone. "Hi, my Danny!"

Her baby was twenty years old already, and in his third year of university. His teenaged interest in political science had never faded, but he'd shifted his focus to social work. Fortunately for Jilly, he'd also decided to stay in Manitoba, so while he wasn't living at home anymore, he was only an hour away. When he could be bothered to come home.

"Hi, Mom. Guess who just aced his first exam of the semester?"

"Way to go. This one..." she looked at the calendar on the fridge, "...Advanced Sociological Research Methods?"

"Yes, it was. And by aced, I mean, I'm pretty sure I might have got a seventy."

"That's awesome, Dan!" Her son had always strug-gled with math and statistics. If it weren't for the fact the class was mandatory for his degree, he never would have taken it. "I guess all that tutoring with Alex paid off."

"It did."

Dan's boyfriend Alex was studying to become an actuary, specializing in Dan's weakest subjects. It never failed to amuse her. "So only three more to go?" Jilly asked.

"Yes, but my last one isn't until the twenty-second in the afternoon. Then we're heading up to Dauphin the next day to celebrate Christmas with Alex's family. We're heading back at six o'clock in the morning on the twenty-sixth, so we'll be at your place for lunch."

"That sounds great, sweetie." It sounded horrible. But, as Dan had reminded her, she'd had the boys on Thanksgiving weekend, which meant Alex hadn't been home since September. Next year she'd magnanimously give up Thanksgiving to have her son home for Christmas.

"You're still making a turkey, right? And your stuffing?"

Actually, she wasn't. "I thought we'd do something different this year and have a Boxing Day Brunch. Maybe with a ham, or a small roasted chicken," she said. Maybe a rotisserie one if she could get one from the grocery store.

"But...but...sage and onion dressing," her son whined.

"Maybe I can whip up some dressing anyway, just for you."

"I'm your favourite son."

"You're my only son," she agreed with a laugh.

They chatted for a few more minutes, talking about what

present he'd found for Alex, and how nuts the malls were. There was a slight pang when she realized she wouldn't be opening his gifts from Santa on Christmas morning, but overall, his call had done her more good than harm. She was about to say goodbye when Dan snuck in one more question.

"Who's Ebenezer?" he asked.

"What?"

"I hear you're seeing some guy named Ebenezer. Is he ninety?"

"No!" she replied before she thought about it.

"Then he does exist. How old is he?"

Jilly couldn't backtrack now. She should have known her son would hear that she'd gone on a date. "Ben is my age. So no more jokes about his age," she warned. "He's single, no kids."

"Wait, Ben? Ben the trucker who drops of his paperwork at our place in the evenings? Brown hair, a bit of salt and pepper going on?" Dan asked. He'd met Ben a few times. Dan had occasionally joined her and Ben when they watched the tail end of a hockey game in the living room. "He seems like a nice guy."

"I like him."

"Hmm, my mom goes for the silver fox type. Have you kissed him yet?"

Her kid was incorrigibly pushy. Just the way she'd taught him to be. "Aren't you supposed to be studying for your next exam?"

"Aw, Mom."

"The sooner you write your exams, the sooner you can go to Alex's for Christmas, and the sooner you can come here for Christmas Day the Sequel," Jilly said.

"Fine, but if Ebenezer doesn't have you home by ten

o'clock on your next date if it's on a workday, he and I are going to have a little chat," Daniel said.

The line went silent, and it wasn't the normal, comfortable silence she was used to sharing with her son. "What's wrong?" she asked.

"Are you alright?"

"Me? I'm fine. A little swamped at work, but that's December."

"No. About me not being home on the twenty-fifth. Waking up and having our stockings and monkey bread and everything. Christmas has always been the two of us. Will you be okay? I hate to think of you all by yourself, especially since even Grandma and Grandpa are gone. I don't want you to be lonely."

Her boy was too sweet. And too worried about a woman who was well able to take care of herself. He'd heard about Ben. She winced when she thought of what he might have heard about the rest of her Grinch-like behaviour. "I was really disappointed, I must admit. But I'm getting over it."

"But what are you going to do on Christmas?"

He *had* heard something. "I'm not sure yet. Sleep in without getting woken up by a son who'd already snuck a handful of chocolates before six in the morning? Make myself a snack board and graze all day? Accept one of the invitations I've received for dinner with friends, or go visiting at the Sunset? The possibilities are endless." She meant her words to be comfort for her son but as she spoke, she recognized the truth in them.

Her Christmas hadn't been cancelled until she cancelled it. She'd have everything that made it worthwhile, it just wouldn't match the calendar date.

"Mom, you went quiet."

"I was thinking it was a good thing your grandparents are out of town. Dad would have sent me to my room for making you feel bad, especially considering how many early and late holidays we celebrated when he had to work on the big days themselves. Hospitals don't keep themselves clean, boyo," Jilly said, mocking her father's accent.

"He definitely would have."

"So I mean it. I'll be fine and waiting to greet you and Alex on the twenty-sixth with sage stuffing and a bird of some kind. Goodbye, Danny."

"Bye, Mom. Love you."

She had to reheat her supper, but she didn't mind. She'd raised a good kid, and hearing from him put her in a better mood. Jilly hoped it lasted through the evening, because although she wasn't certain what she was going to walk into at the Sunset, she was certain it would keep her up all night.

CHAPTER 10

BEN INTENDED to wolf down some soup and a sandwich after Sprite's extra-long, after-work walk before he loaded them both into his car to head to the auditions, but a call from his mother changed that plan. Instead, his across-the-street puppy sitter agreed to take Sprite for a couple hours, and Ben changed into a nice shirt in anticipation of meeting his mother for supper after her last-minute invitation.

Anything but liver and onions, he thought to himself as he watched the first residents file into the communal dining room. When he saw the week's menu posted outside the doors, he smiled. Liver and onions had been an option the night before.

That was how his mother found him. She stood beside him to look at the menu as well, and immediately began to laugh. "No, you missed the liver and onions," she told him. "So did I. They ran out."

"I do not understand old people. Why would anyone order that?" he demanded.

"Good taste?" She laughed again, and familiar warmth washed over him. "Let's eat."

She looked good. Residents weren't required to dress up for meals, but there was a minimum dress code for the dining room, so nobody showed up in their bathrobes. Ben noticed her nails were a bright red, probably thanks to the on-site salon. He was thrilled to see her take advantage of it, since his mother had been too shaky to do her own lately, and the times he had tried he'd made a mess of it.

She introduced him to two tables full of people before they took their own seats. The waitress greeted her by name and knew her drink order before she gave it, and more people came over to say hello throughout their meal. "You're pretty popular. You've made a lot of friends," Ben noted.

"Some are new, but a lot of them have been friends for years. When I moved in, I was able to slide back into my old bridge club, since so many of them are living here. I couldn't get out to play when I was in the house."

He noticed she didn't say "when I was at home."

Ben ordered the chicken pot pie, while his mother ordered the meatless lasagna. She was right; they were tasty meals, and better quality than anything she could have reheated or prepared for herself on her own. She had friends. She had most of her old furniture, which easily filled her one-bedroom suite. She was happy, despite his guilt.

He didn't know what to do with that.

Or the conversation she'd just started.

"I hear you've been seeing a new woman since you started your new job," his mother said as he stuffed a forkful of crust and chicken into mouth.

"You did?" he choked out over the flaky pastry crust.

"We're a bunch of old, liver-loving folks with nothing better to do than gossip, Ebenezer. Who is she?"

How did he describe Jilly Lewis to his mother? "She's divorced, with a son in university. She's an executive assistant, and good at her job. She has an extensive collection of Christmas décor." He though for another minute. "She likes to knit. And cats. And rollercoasters. Jilly loves rollercoasters."

"Is she pretty?"

"Yes. Very."

"Blonde?"

"Brunette." The colour of wet sand on a sunny day. Short, with a tendency to stick out.

"Blue eyes?"

"Brown." Like the too-bitter cocoa she liked to offer him when he came over.

"Short?"

"Tall." Tall enough to almost look him in the eyes in her work heels. He had to tilt his head down when they were at her place.

"I guess I'll see for myself soon enough," his mom said.

"What?"

"Flora said she'd be here tonight. I'll check her out then."

"Mother!"

"Eat your cauliflower. I see it hiding in the gravy."

By the time he finished dessert, Ben no longer had any qualms about the quality of food his mom was receiving. He also appreciated the fact she was no longer stuck doing dishes. Maybe there were advantages to her being here he'd been unwilling to see.

She excused herself, saying she needed to get something from her room, so he kissed her cheek goodnight, and headed to Flora Mercado's office.

The tiny recreation director led him to a main-floor leisure area they had to themselves. Jilly arrived a moment later, and Flora directed them to a pair of chairs in front of a small wood-floored area at one side of the carpeted room. The card tables, which were usually by the window, had been pushed into a corner. Other chairs were arranged behind theirs, like audience seating. Then Flora opened the door and residents began to filter in. More than twelve of them. Ben leaned closer to Jilly. "They're taking this awfully seriously," he said quietly, as the chairs behind them began to fill.

"We are in so much trouble," she agreed.

Flora walked to the middle of the wooden floor. "Thank you, Jilly and Ben, for coming on such short notice. I'd hoped for a couple volunteers, but the response was so overwhelming, we had to respond accordingly. We have eleven acts to audition for you tonight. They will be demonstrating their Christmas skills to earn a spot on the town's float. First up is Mr. Wojowitz and his amazing handkerchiefs."

Ben took a deep breath. "What have you gotten me into?" he whispered.

"Shut up and clap," Jilly ordered, as a man who had to be at least eighty walked jauntily onto the stage.

The bald senior in the Christmas sweater pulled three neon handkerchiefs from his suit jacket pocket, one at a time, fluffing them with a showman's flair. "I could do this and wave from the float at the same time. I think the kids would be impressed with a juggling Santa," he informed them. With that, he threw them up in the air, and the light cloths floated down gently before he grabbed them and tossed them up again. After a thirty-second demonstration, he tucked all the handkerchiefs back in his pocket and took a bow.

"Thank you, Mr. Wojowitz, that was very impressive," Flora said after the applause died. "Next up is Mr. Parker and his magic tricks."

"You owe me so much for this," Ben said under his breath as he clapped for the next act.

There was the magician, followed by a portly man who did nothing but grab his stomach and say "Ho, Ho, Ho!" But he did it with a lot of jolliness, Ben noted on the clipboard Flora had provided.

Then they got to the Mrs. Clauses. Two of them wore red dresses, and three of them had white hair. Four of them sang, and Ben had to jump to his feet to convince two of them it was okay if they both auditioned with "Up on the Rooftop."

As he settled back in his chair, Jilly turned to him. Her grin startled him. "Didn't you want to watch an octogenarian slap fight?"

"No!"

She smiled wider. In fact, her smile grew with each new person in front of them. After the last lady left the stage, Ben glanced over his shoulder. The back of the room was standing room only, which explained why the applause seemed to grow after each act.

He had to recuse himself when the seventh woman took the stage. "Mom?" he asked in disbelief.

"Don't distract me or you'll go on the naughty list, Ebenezer!" And then his mother, who he had watched slowly become reclusive over the last few years, not wanting to leave the house for anything except grocery shopping and church, do a little dance. Not just a dance; she also had a ribbon on a stick that she waved around the room.

He had no idea what to say, but he clapped extra hard after Jilly elbowed him in the ribs. He barely saw the final act.

"Thank you very much, everyone," Flora said. "Jilly and Ben will have the results to you..."

"Tomorrow evening," Jilly said. "After that, we'll get started right away on the costume fittings. Thank you, everyone, for going to so much effort tonight. We truly appreciate it. It'll be a difficult choice, but the whole town will hear about how many Mr. and Mrs. Clauses offered their services for the parade."

She sounded sincere. He had no idea how real it was until they were alone in the parking lot. "They were all really invested in getting on the float," Jilly commented. Her toque was yanked low over her forehead, and her scarf was pulled high, leaving only her eyes visible.

"I didn't expect that kind of response either," he said.

"They prepared songs and dances and did magic tricks. This meant something."

"Do you have any favourites?"

"I was partial to Mr. Wojowitz. Not that he'll be able to juggle on the float, but he was pretty spry. I think he'd be a good St. Nick."

"I agree. How about Mrs. Claus?"

"I'm not sure. Mrs. Malek had a great voice, but I don't think I'd want to see her outside for two hours on a float. She had a slight cough."

"Mrs. Fredericks?" he asked.

She winced. "I really want to say yes for you, but she looked a little...frail? Unsteady? I don't think I'd want her on a float for the same reasons as Mrs. Malek. Are you mad?"

"Not at all." Honestly, he was a little relieved. Jilly was right. His mom had the right attitude, but it would be a physically demanding night, and he wasn't sure she had it in her. The desire, yes; the strength, not so much.

"She was really cute though. Do you know why she kept winking at me?"

He knew exactly why. His mom was signaling to everyone in the room that she approved of his girlfriend. Not that he'd ever admit it in this lifetime. "No idea whatsoever."

Jilly continued, oblivious. "I think Mrs. Johnson would get a kick out of doing her royal wave. Plus, Mr. Johnson passed away a year ago last winter, so I'd like to get her involved since she offered."

He shouldn't have been surprised Jilly knew the residents, even if she didn't have family there.

Then she added, "Thanks for coming tonight. Now I can hand this project back to Nick and be done with it."

Just when he thought her heart was thawing.

CHAPTER 11

JILLY KNEW she hadn't had the best attitude for the last couple weeks, but she never thought her mood would be the reason she was out of a job. She'd shown up at the church at nine o'clock on a Saturday morning, ready to work, and they had the nerve to try to send her home.

"Thank you so much for bringing these," Helen Gauthier exclaimed when Jilly tromped down the stairs carefully carrying four bags of knit goods. "You can drop them on the table. There will be a lot of happy, warm tootsies on the twenty-fifth," she noted happily.

"Where do you want me?" It had been a long time since Jilly had pulled out her calligraphy set. She'd traditionally had the best and easiest job of the afternoon: the gift-tag-writer-in-chief. As the other member of the gifts for seniors committee sorted and wrapped all the donated presents, they would bring her the beribboned packages and confirm the contents. Then Jilly wrote out a nametag and secured it to the gift bags.

"You're free to go," Helen said. The December native, and a nurse practitioner at the hospital, took her arm and walked her back to the steps that led to the main floor of the United Church.

"What?"

"We have lots of volunteers here today, and I know you aren't up to extra holiday tasks this year. We appreciate you taking the time to drop off the bags. It saves us from sending someone to collect them. But we won't keep you for the rest of the morning."

"Now, wait a minute," Jilly protested. She'd been volunteering with this charity for six years, ever since she'd taken up knitting after her fortieth birthday. They weren't going to shoo her out the door at the good part. Making the gift was enjoyable but giving it away was the fun part.

"We don't want to put you out," Helen explained. "Your donations are more than generous, and we don't want you to feel pressured. Amanda Hill has offered to take over the labelling."

This was ridiculous. Yes, Jilly had said she didn't want to celebrate Christmas. But she never said she'd run around snatching all the wreaths off the doors in town either. "I'd like to be part of this. We've done a lot of work all year. I'd like to see it through." Whipping off a pair of slippers took her about a week. But the committee wasn't all knitting all the time. The Southern Manitoba Fibre Association also held two fundraisers, at Easter and Thanksgiving, where they sold donated items to raise money to buy the Christmas presents they needed. Jilly's baby jackets and Joy's fingerless mittens had proven to be very popular at both.

She wasn't about to go home now.

"No, I insist. I brought my good nibs and my ink bottle, and I'm ready to go. We don't have a lot of time to do this all, so let's get to work," Jilly said with false cheer.

Helen's mouth opened and closed a couple times, but she eventually acquiesced. "Let's get you set up at the end table, so you'll have room to write."

Jilly jumped right in. She only waited for a minute before the first gift bag appeared in front of her. She overheard conversations going on around her, which were mostly holiday related, but nobody spoke to her or tried to draw her into them. It hurt a little. She'd known these women and their children for years.

Adelaide Klassen seemed to be over her cold, although she choked out a cough whenever she noticed Jilly looking at her. It confirmed Jilly's suspicion that Adelaide and her grandson had set her up to make her work on the float. Getting even with Nick would be easy enough; she ought to be able to feed him decaf for about three mornings in a row before he caught on. Adelaide was going to be harder, but Jilly would get her revenge eventually.

The others avoided her too. Jilly wanted to hear where Amanda managed to score the hot toy her daughter wanted, and how they were planning to disguise their kids' annual new pajama gifts. Joy was excited about her husband Decker's former cop partner coming out for a visit over the holidays. But whenever they noticed her listening in, they smiled and lowered their voices or changed the subject.

Yes, she'd been more than clear about her feelings for Christmas this year. Now it was biting her in the butt. But since she couldn't get mad about them doing what she'd insisted upon, she'd have to make the uncomfortable move of admitting she'd overreacted and that she wanted to hear about other people's holiday plans so long as they didn't ask her about her own. All she had to do was figure out how.

Although they had almost six dozen knit and crocheted pieces of clothing, it didn't take very long to go through the piles with five people doing the wrapping. "Helen, Joy told me you needed us for three hours today, but we're almost done already," Jilly said. She pointed at the now-empty bags she'd carried to the basement to emphasize her point.

"This is round one, Jilly. I'm expecting a delivery any time," Helen said.

Heavy footsteps fell on the stairs.

"And here it is," she continued.

Jilly didn't recognize the boots, or the jeans. But when the rest of Ben came into view, she burst into a smile.

He'd been hard to find since the night of the audition. She couldn't blame him, not after he saw her reaction to Joy, and then how she acted when she learned about the Claus auditions. He was trying to make things festive for his mother's first holiday out of her house, and Jilly had made it perfectly clear she wanted nothing to do with such efforts.

Although she would have helped him do *that*. Mrs. Fredericks's first Christmas in a new place deserved to be extra-special, since it would likely to be extra-hard. Jilly had been trying to find a way to approach Ben to offer her expertise, but she hadn't come up with anything yet.

But now, here he was. "What on earth?" she asked.

"I know I haven't been around much lately. I asked around and got some things donated to fill the holes on your list. Now you can save your money for the stuff I couldn't find." He hefted the bags in his hands. "Where I can I set these? I have another load upstairs."

Jilly and Helen quickly cleared a spot on a table and were unpacking before Ben hit the stairs. Boxes of hand cream and fancy soaps, large-print hardback mysteries, puzzle books, jigsaw puzzles. Jilly had no idea where he'd acquired everything; she didn't recognize most of the brand names. He returned with another load. She ignored the stack of wrapped gifts at her station to see what else he'd found. Insulated, spill-proof coffee cups, stained glass starburst window decorations, and wheelchair pouches. "These are incredible. Where did you get it all?"

"I know every small shop from Winnipeg west to Vancouver and south to Florida. I made some calls and sent some emails, asking if anyone had anything they'd like to donate for a good cause, and had trucker friends make some stops to pick them up. They've been dropping them off at the warehouse all week. I hope they help."

"Help? These are perfect. People will love them." He'd managed to find about half the items they needed. They'd have more than enough in their budget to cover the rest.

"That's good to hear. Do you need another set of hands for wrapping?"

They really didn't. The other ladies were working like a well-oiled machine. But Jilly didn't want him to leave either. "I could use a double checker. Can you confirm the gifts to the names on the list, and sort them into delivery piles? Most are going to the Sunset, but we have a few going to the care home in Carman, and a few are for shut-ins in the area." She knew full well which packages were heading to other destinations. Years of experience had taught the group to colour code the gift wrap as an extra precaution. But Ben didn't know that.

"Can do," he said.

"Helen, did Ben mention what we were up to the other night at the Sunset?" Jilly called across the room.

"Bingo?" was her friend's guess.

"No. We were auditioning Mr. and Mrs. Clauses for the town float. With my parents out of town, we needed to fill those famous red suits. Rather than hiring actors, Ben came up with the idea of asking some of the residents if they'd be interested. We had a dozen people show up to volunteer. Their enthusiasm shocked the pants off me." Jilly smiled when she spoke, trying to put extra cheer into her words to show she was impressed with the seniors' efforts.

"You're working on the town float?" Joy sounded horrified at the idea.

"It was Nick's idea."

"No further explanation needed." But Joy gave a tiny smile when she made the comment. Jilly hoped that meant she'd be open to an apology later, because she owed her a big one.

"We have the costume fittings this week, which doesn't leave us much time since the parade is next week-end. I can't believe it's the middle of the month already," Jilly continued.

"My daughter is looking forward to it. She's missed the last couple years," Amanda said. "We've already told her we're bundling her in a million blankets. Madison called us overprotective, but all that got her was a million and one blankets." Her short black curls bounced as she shrugged unrepentantly.

"That's understandable." Helen had been the one to

organize the weekly casserole drop-offs to the Hills while their daughter had been undergoing chemotherapy a couple years ago.

"Not only is Dan missing the parade this year because of exams, but he isn't coming home for Christmas either," Jilly said. She might as well put it in the open. "He'll be here on Boxing Day, but it's the first year he's missed the twenty-fifth. I'm not handling it well."

"Oh, honey, the first Christmas without the kids is always the hardest," Helen said sympathetically.

"Thank goodness I have a few more years before that happens," Amanda added.

"Tell us more about those auditions," Joy requested. "Were there any good acts?"

"There was an octogenarian slap fight. Almost," Ben said.

And the whole tone of the room shifted. Jilly didn't participate much. Aside from describing the acts, she didn't have much to add. She couldn't talk about her decorating or baking since she didn't have any, but at least the others weren't scared of her anymore.

Now she needed to make two more specific apologies. She needed a place to start and a moment to do it, but it would all have to wait until after the parade.

The delay did, however, give her a chance to ensure she did a good job when the time was right.

CHAPTER 12

THERE WAS something wrong with her car heater. It had barely worked enough to defrost her windshield. There was nothing left to heat the interior. She was chilled to the bone. Jilly pulled a frozen block of borscht out of the freezer and put it in the microwave to defrost. Nothing warmed her faster than a big bowl of steaming hot soup. She savoured every spoonful, and then sopped up the remaining pink liquid at the bottom of the bowl with a well buttered piece of crusty bun. She felt human by the time she was done.

She was settling in for an evening of yarn and home-renovation binge-watching when her phone binged with an incoming text. She received two more before she retrieved it from the charging station in the kitchen.

Sprite puked a little. Do puppies do that sometimes?

Sprite just puked a lot. Do puppy tummies hold that much?

Do you have any spare paper towels?

Jilly had no idea you could hear "frantic" through a text. She bypassed the teeny tiny screen keyboard and dialed directly. "Is she still throwing up?" she asked as soon as Ben answered the phone.

"I don't know how she could. I think she's already emptied her stomach twice."

His voice sounded funny. "Are you plugging your nose?" she asked.

"No. Of course not. Do you have paper towels?"

"I'll be right over." Coat, scarf, hat, reusable grocery bag with two rolls of paper towels, boots, and mitts. Getting dressed in the winter was half a workout in itself, she thought as she caught her breath. Rather than start the car and wait for it to warm up, and then drive the few blocks to Ben's apartment, Jilly decided it would be faster to walk it. The snow squeaked under her soles when she pranced in place waiting for the crosswalk light to change.

A brusque "It's open" answered her knock on Ben's door. She opened it carefully, mindful of any knee-high occupants who might be trying to make a break for freedom. Instead, she was greeted with a wet, beleaguered Ben holding a squirming puppy in one hand and a dripping towel in the other.

Jilly blinked twice. "Into to the tub. Both of you." By the time she stripped off her winter wear, Ben and Sprite were in the tub. The dog yipped at the cold porcelain on its paws. Ben just stood there, his shoulders stooped.

"Do you have another towel for the dog?" she asked.

"There's another striped one in the linen closet in the hall."

Jilly found the big striped bath towel on the centre shelf. She wet the corner of it in the bathroom sink, and carefully wiped around Sprite's mouth, the fur on her chest, and her feet. Then she bundled the puppy into the rest of it and snuggled her against her chest. "How dirty are you?" she asked quietly.

"My shirt. My socks. Both my socks. I found the first puddle with my foot," Ben said with a grimace. His sweat-pants legs were pulled up above his calves, while his formerly white sport socks were bunched around his ankles.

"I'll take the dog. You get changed. I recommend you rinse the clothes in the tub until you can get them into the washer." She had twenty years' experience of sick kids and cats. Her heart ached a little at the scared look that flashed across Ben's face every time he looked at Sprite, shivering in her arms. "She'll be okay. We'll wait for you in the living room."

Sprite whined and wiggled in her lap as they both waited for Ben to reappear. When he did, he was in jeans, a charcoal grey Henley, socks, and running shoes. But better than that, he had a small smile on his face. "Okay. I can do this. One step at a time." He looked at Jilly hope-fully. "What's the first step?"

"Cleaning up the mess while answering a couple questions," she said. She offered him the puppy, but he waved her off, insisting she stay on the sofa while he tore open the roll of paper towels and got to work.

It was Jilly's first time in Ben's apartment, and she had no shame about looking around while he was distracted. He had a new television, with a full sound system set-up, and a gaming system on a lower shelf of the console stand. Framed nature prints hung over his sofa and on the wall of his combination kitchen/dining area. The apartment was painted in various shades of beige, but Ben's heavy furniture—leather couch and coarse plaid-covered easy chair—gave it desperately needed texture.

What really surprised her was the three-foot Christmas tree on his kitchen table. It took up half of the area and was decorated with a string of tiny white lights, and thumb-sized gold ornaments. It even sat on its own poinsettia-patterned placemat. The tree was visible from every corner of the apartment, and it added a welcome, warm glow.

"Did you contact a vet after Sprite got sick?" she asked.

"Yes. The vet said to keep an eye on her and call back if it happened again. But she's been okay for the last twenty minutes," Ben said. "The vet gave me a whole list of things dogs can't eat. I didn't feed Sprite any of them. No chocolate, no grapes, no chicken bones."

Soon the scent of pine and antiseptic added to the apartment's ambience. "Maybe she got into something on her own," Jilly said. "Can we take a look around?" Sprite was dozing off in her arms. Jilly shifted the puppy off her lap and made a nest out of the towel and a blanket hanging from the back of the sofa.

Crawling around the floor on their hands and knees, looking for things a puppy could have accidentally gotten into, was pretty undignified. But they were undignified together. Ben kept looking over at her and smiling.

"A-ha!" Jilly pulled out two crumpled tinfoil wrappers from beneath the sofa. "Could she have unwrapped and eaten these chocolates?"

Ben's cheeks turned red, and it wasn't because he was practically standing on his head. "No, those were my Christmas bells. I like to enjoy a few chocolates when I'm watching TV. Those wrappers got away from me last night."

"You eat no-name chocolates and enjoy them?" Jilly

was stunned, and a little saddened. Treats needed to be savoured, not choked down and leaving a powdery after-taste. "My friend, we have to introduce you to the world of quality chocolate."

"Jilly, sometimes you need the cheap chocolate. The processed mac-and-cheese. The pimento loaf sandwich—"

"Nobody needs pimento loaf, Ben. *Ever*."

Their search continued unsuccessfully, turning up fewer dust bunnies than Jilly would have found in her own house, until they reached the kitchen. "I think I found your problem," Jilly announced.

"What?"

She felt her shoulders drop in relief. "Dog food."

Ben stood up, straightening and stretching his back in a way Jilly knew all too well. "It can't be. That's the brand the vet and Penny recommended."

Jilly twisted the bag, so he could see the large hole gnawed in the back, and the kibble that was spilled onto the kitchen floor. "I think Sprite decided to choose her own portion size."

He gasped. "That bag was three-quarters full this morning!"

The bag was down to half. "Her eyes were bigger than her stomach, but she gave it the old college try." No wonder the poor thing had a tummy ache.

She swept up the spilled food and poured the rest into an ice cream pail Ben dug out of his kitchen cupboards while he called the vet. Five minutes later, the dog food was safely out of reach on top of the fridge, and Ben was rummaging through an upper cabinet. She thought her visit was over since the mystery was solved, but realized Ben had other ideas when he pulled out two wine glasses. "Would you like to join me?" he asked.

She took the glasses and he pulled a bottle of wine from the fridge. They each took a seat on either side of Sprite, who was now snoozing on the sofa. She held out the glasses, and he carefully poured the wine, not spilling a drop even though he was stretched over a cushion and a puppy.

The wine took the edge off what started as a frightening, frantic evening. Jilly relaxed into the sofa and sipped the fruity red wine. She reached across the furry divide and patted Ben's arm before letting her mind drift in the easy silence.

***

Between the stress of wondering what was wrong with Sprite and crawling around on the floor for half an hour, Ben's heart was pounding like he'd run a marathon. Jilly was a blessing and he was grateful for her. Now his puppy was sleeping like a baby and Jilly had her stockinged feet on his coffee table as they enjoyed a glass of wine.

Ben stretched his arm out across the back of the sofa. The tips of his fingers brushed the tips of Jilly's flyaway curls. He could see more of this in his future, a lot more. Quiet evenings with Jilly, hanging out at home, or doing something around town. Taking Sprite for walks in the snow, or longer walks past green trees and flower gardens in the summer. "Do you have good walking shoes?" he asked. Then he realized she had no context for the out-of-the-blue question.

"I'll need to break in a new pair in the spring. My

boots are only a year old, though. They can stand up to a few walks around the block. Or town, depending on whether or not you find Sprite's off-switch." She slowly turned her head to look at him. "Or were you not talking about walking the dog together?"

"No, that's exactly what I was talking about."

She dropped her head forward, and he moved his arm so he could rub her exposed neck. "I didn't think I'd see you again after you stopped driving."

He snorted in laughter, almost spilling his wine. Jilly pulled away from him, her face carefully blank. "I didn't know I was being funny."

He was surprised she hadn't caught on yet. "When I parked my rig for the last time, one of the reasons was to spend more time with you. I wanted more than an hour or two after a run. Although I was hoping it would be more relaxing than it has been. We seem to be running from one crisis to another these days. I was hoping for more date nights and fewer emergency call outs."

"We have had more than our fair share of those, haven't we?"

"I don't mind, but this"—he raised his wine glass and gestured at the two of them relaxing on his sofa—"is much better."

"It is."

She took a sip of wine, but choked on it. "Wait a minute. Did you say that I was one of the reasons you quit driving?"

Ben knew he had it bad when even her slowness was cute. "I wanted to be in December more because my mom is getting older. But I wanted more time with you too, and I figured I needed to make the first move."

Jilly gave the blanket Sprite was snoozing on a tug.

The puppy roused herself, jumped off, and toddled to her dog bed, where she quickly resettled herself and fell back asleep. Then Jilly gathered up the towel and blanket and piled it on the coffee table. She scooted closer to him. "Then don't you think it's time you made that move?"

He deliberately set his glass on the table and turned to face her. He'd been looking forward to this for a while. "I do," he said, before he leaned in for a kiss.

CHAPTER 13

IT WAS A BEAUTIFUL, clear night. Thankfully it was also still, because even a slight breeze would have dropped the temperature to unbearably cold levels. As it was, the people of December grinned at each other behind their scarves and said, "Yes, it is a little nippy tonight," and then took a sip of their coffee or hot chocolate or whatever they held in their insulated cups as they waited along the sides of Main Street and the other roads along the short parade route.

Ben had ensured his mother had a prime seat by the windows in the second-floor common room which overlooked the Sunset Retirement Residence parking lot. There wasn't a spare viewing spot, and he knew the main floor was equally packed. He appreciated that the parade committee scheduled a loop through the residence and hospital parking lots so those who couldn't come out could still participate in a small way. She was settled in with a hot chocolate and a gigantic gingerbread cookie which Ben had brought her from the Pumpkin Patch's dessert display case.

Once he was certain she was set up, he hurried down the block to the high school parking lot where the parade committee was marshaling the floats.

The fire truck was the first in line, simply draped in garland in case they were called out on an emergency. Its flashing red light was advanced warning for those up the street that the fun was about to start.

The United Church and Greenjeans grocery store shared a pickup truck. The vehicle was covered in Christmas lights, and the box was stuffed with goodies for the volunteers to distribute to spectators on the sidewalks. Packets of hot chocolate and soup mix, bags of chips, and Christmas chocolates were handed out with abandon.

The carolers were next. They weren't from the school or from the church. It was whoever had shown up at the four practices preceding the parade. Their set list included all the classics, *O Tannenbaum* in German, *Feliz Navidad* in Spanish, and a rousing version of *I Want a Hippopotamus for Christmas*. They were on foot, and probably grateful the entire event was only twenty blocks long.

The North Pole Unlimited display was next. The float rolled down the street behind Clementine, Nick Klassen's 1940s pickup truck. The whole town recognized the classic vehicle, and it was perfect for this event, down to its cherry-red paint. The entire visual effect was stunning. While Ben knew it was the same base as the summer parade float, the lights and decorations made it unrecognizable.

"Did you do that?" Ben asked Jilly, who'd come back to the shelter of the gym wall after finishing the Klassen float.

"Yep."

"How?"

"Magic," she said.

"It must be." Two workshop stations on either side of trailer deck had elves working away at their various tasks, from gift wrapping to toy testing. In the middle was an elf boss who yelled "Get to work, we're on a deadline, people!" whenever he saw one of the elves waving to people in the crowd. The folks on the sidelines loved it.

Ben squinted. "Is the elf boss wearing a nametag that says Nick?" he asked.

"Maybe."

One local farmer had decorated his tractor, and another had a horse-drawn wagon filled with waving Christmas movie characters. After that came a light display of different wire-framed animals on a flatbed trailer pulled by Eve LeBlanc's wreath-adorned tow truck.

Then came the float they'd all been waiting for. Santa himself, accompanied by Mrs. Claus. A bag full of presents threatened to spill out of the back of the sleigh if the lone reindeer with his red nose took a corner too quickly, but it looked like the real deal. Mr. Wojowitz bounced in his seat as he turned and shouted "ho, ho, ho" to each individual person, the pillow strapped to his stomach not impeding his mobility in any way. His long white beard flapped in his face with his constant motion, but he didn't seem to mind. Mrs. Johnson, with her natural white curls peeking out from beneath her cherry-red cap, was the picture of serenity as she waved to the crowd.

"They look great," Ben said. "Are they okay in the cold?"

Jilly nodded. "They both have electric lap blankets,

and a walkie talkie in case they want to quit early. But I don't think either of them will."

"Me, neither."

Since there were only a dozen vehicles, the anticipation, parade, and disbursement only lasted an hour. Ben's thick socks, long johns, and the pants tucked into his winter boots made him feel like he was walking like a bow-legged Yeti, but he wasn't cold. Ben and Jilly helped the Clauses off the float, and into the car that was waiting to take them back to the Sunset.

"Do you have to collect the costumes tonight?"

"No, that's a job for another day." The corners of her mouth turned up. "Besides, I have a sneaking suspicion they might want to wear them to the late-night coffee time and show off a little."

He could see that. "I'm guessing they'll take advantage of the bragging rights until next Christmas. You may have started a new tradition. Your parents could be out of luck when they get back from their trip." He didn't tell Jilly that, according to his mother, some of the residents were already planning their acts for the auditions next December. He didn't think she was ready to hear that yet.

"Are you ready to head out?" Jilly asked.

"Yes. I walked. By the time I found a spot, I'd be parked in front of my place anyway."

"Me too. Want to come to my place for a drink to warm you up before you head home?"

He didn't have a chance to respond before they were interrupted by a cheerful blonde. "Hi, Jilly. Hi, Jilly's friend."

"Ben Fredericks, may I introduce Eve LeBlanc, tow-truck driver and my boss's fiancée. Eve, this is Ben from the NPU's Logistics team."

"And Jilly's boyfriend," he added, offering his mittened hand in greeting.

"Please don't tell me Clementine broke down along the parade route," Jilly begged.

"No, she's fine. I was talking to Nick and my mom, and I wanted to invite you to our December 24th open house movie marathon at my mom's house," Eve said. "I'm on call all day, but we'll be running them from about nine in the morning till bedtime, which is also about nine. Mom said your family was out of town this year, so I wanted you to know you're welcome any time."

Ben flinched. It was a generous offer from a friend, but Eve's casualness about Jilly's situation was blunt enough to border on harsh. He looked at Jilly, waiting to see how she reacted.

"You know, that sounds like more fun than sitting home alone. I can bring a Crockpot full of cocoa and some snacks," Jilly offered, surprising the pants off him.

"Wow, that sounds great!"

"Can I bring a friend?"

"Who?" he asked, not caring he was interrupting their conversation.

"You, genius."

"Oh."

Eve guffawed. "Sure. As we said, the more, the merrier. Please be warned that although Mom and I have tried, my sister still insists that *Star Wars* is a Christmas movie, so that will be one of the options at some point." The blonde shrugged. "I guess any movie is a Christmas movie with enough shortbread cookies. My choices include *A Christmas Story* and *Die Hard*, which is undoubtedly the best Christmas movie ever."

"Isn't that the truth," Ben agreed.

Jilly was entering Eve's party into her phone's calendar when they were interrupted again by a young girl shouting, "Eve! Eve!" Then the shouts changed to a much more urgent, "Bucky! Bucky, no!"

Then disaster struck. Specifically, it bounced off Eve and struck Jilly, knocking her to the ground. A large, excited golden retriever danced around Jilly's prone body, yelping excitedly. Its headband sported felt reindeer antlers that bounced along in time. Eve grabbed the dog and pulled it away, while Ben knelt to help Jilly.

"Are you okay?"

"No."

He reached for her arm, and she batted him away with her other hand. "Not the arm!" she cried.

He saw a sheen of tears in her eyes that had nothing to do with the cold air. "What's wrong with it?"

"I landed on it. Badly."

It took a moment to get Jilly back on her feet. In the meantime, a young girl had rushed over, leash in hand. "I'm sorry," Madison Hill cried. "Bucky's collar broke. He didn't mean it."

"Accidents happen. It's not your fault, Madison," Jilly said. She was trying to be kind, but Ben heard the strain in her voice.

Eve managed to fashion a halter around the dog out of an extra-long scarf, and she wrapped the leash around it to let Madison pull the dog away.

"Do you want to ice it at home, or are we looking at a trip to the hospital?" he asked.

"Hospital."

He bundled her into the passenger seat and let her fumble with the seatbelt one-handed before she leaned back and asked for his help with an exasperated grunt.

"Did you hurt anything besides your arm when you landed?"

"Besides my pride? No. I twisted on purpose to land on my left side because I'm right-handed. I hope it's not broken. That's all I need a week before Christmas."

The hospital was dead quiet when they drove up to the emergency room doors. Helen Gauthier looked up from the nursing station when they walked in. "What happened? No ambulance? I didn't get a call."

"Jilly got bowled over at the parade by an exuberant spectator and landed badly on her left arm," Ben said.

"Okay, let's take a look," Helen said.

Her examination didn't take long and revealed bruising and a sprained wrist. Helen quickly had Jilly set up with a wrist brace and a sling, and a prescribed course of action consisting of ice, aspirin, and a moratorium on knitting until the new year.

The last proclamation elicited the biggest response. "Come on, Helen, be reasonable."

"Organize your yarn stash. Count all your double pointed needles. Take up crochet. Just don't knit."

"Someone is getting coal in her stocking for Christmas. I can arrange that because Eve invited me to your place on Christmas Eve for your movies. Although now, I'll be more of a liability than anything," Jilly added.

"You won't be a liability. I'm so glad you said yes!" Helen exclaimed.

"But I won't be able to bring my cocoa Crockpot or any baking unless Ben wants to carry it for me."

"We'll work something out." He was just thrilled she wasn't cancelling. He was certain being thrown for a loop would have thrown her improving mindset for a loop as well.

Helen's cell phone rang, and she glanced at the screen but ignored it and continued to help Jilly get her now-fat arm into her coat sleeve. "You can answer that," Jilly said. "I'm fine now."

"It's only Eve. I'll call her later."

"She's probably calling to check up on me. She was there when it happened."

"Is it okay if I give her an update?" Helen asked. Her brown eyes, the same shade as her daughter's, were full of concern.

"Of course. Ask her if I'm still invited for the movie marathon if I argue that the best Christmas movie ever is *A Christmas Carol* with Alastair Sim."

Ben took over zipping Jilly's jacket and winding her scarf around her, while Helen called her daughter back. Helen's conversation was short. "Yes, she's here. She'll be fine. She has a sprained wrist, but nothing is broken."

Ben was at the door, with Jilly trailing along behind, when they both stopped, hearing Helen make a pained noise. When they turned around, they saw the nurse practitioner turning an alarming shade of tomato red.

"Are you alright?" Jilly asked.

Helen nodded, then choked out, "I'll call you back" before she dropped her phone on the desk. It took her a minute, but she eventually said, "Why didn't you tell me?"

"Tell you what?" Jilly asked.

"You said you were in an accident."

"I was."

"You didn't say what kind. Or what Bucky was wearing."

Ben looked at Jilly, who appeared as confused as he was. Aside from the golden retriever not wearing a collar because it had broken, he didn't see how that was relevant. "What kind of accident was it?" he asked cautiously.

Helen made that sound again, and blurted out, "Jilly got run over by a rein-dog, walking home with plans for Christmas Eve."

"So?" he asked.

"She's a walking, talking Christmas carol!"

CHAPTER 14

HER HOUSE WAS clean and organized, or as close as she could get with one hand out of commission. Jilly pushed the containers of tree ornaments to the wall and put the fir boughs and lights on the fireplace mantle to get them off the floor. Then she needed to tidy the coffee table, so she tucked the various picture frames and candle holders in the greenery. It looked surprisingly good for something that wasn't a real Christmas decoration.

But more importantly, now she had most of her living room back. She set the coffee table with plates, cutlery, and wine glasses, and switched on her electric fireplace. She lit a couple of candles that had wooden wicks which made the crackling sound the fake fire lacked. All that was missing was dinner and her date.

Ben had been amazing. For the last four days, he'd driven her to and from work, shoveled her driveway, and gone grocery shopping for her. All he'd let her do was point at the items on the shelves, but he'd put them in the cart and carried them from the store to the car and from the car to her kitchen table. She drew the line at him putting them away for her. She could manage one can at a time.

He'd been so great that she'd invited him over for dinner despite her new disability. Ben tried to put her off, but she insisted.

She had a plan. She also still owed him a real apology. The night Sprite got sick, she'd been too concerned with other things to remember to do it, and there hadn't been a good, private moment at the parade.

Ben promised to bring wine and dessert and left the meal up to her. She'd known what they'd be eating before she issued the invitation. Fortunately, of the two cars driving down her street, Ben pulled into her driveway first. The second vehicle pulled in right behind him.

"It's okay, come in," she yelled to Ben when he looked at the other car in concern. She ushered him past the door and into the hall, then waited for her second guest to arrive. That younger man didn't make it past her door. She simply took her proffered offering and sent him on his way.

Ben had one hand on the living doorframe as he took off his boot. "You know, you didn't have to cook for me at all, especially since you're hurt. I would have been happy to take you to..." His voice trailed off when he looked up. "Oh."

"I wanted to cook for you, but that won't be happening anytime soon, and I still wanted to invite you over for dinner. This was my compromise. I hope you don't mind."

"Who minds pizza?"

"I was hoping you'd say that."

Jilly had been wanting another proper date with Ben from the moment they got home from the Prairie Grill, but the timing hadn't worked. She'd planned to invite him over for a nice, home-cooked meal after the parade, but that idea went out the window when she was unable to butter a piece of toast without assistance. Instead, she did the next best thing and arranged a meal she didn't have to cook.

It was a little sneaky, but then again, so was Ben. Arranging for Joy to come see her about a cat. Collecting all the donations for the seniors' Christmas present packages. Slipping a package of cinnamon buns and a box of strawberry Poptarts into her shopping cart, and then distracting her when they went through the checkout, so she didn't find them until she was unpacking at home. And now, bringing over a white poinsettia in addition to a bottle of red and a familiar white, embossed box. Jilly didn't know what to gush over first.

"I swear I'm not pushing the holidays on you," he said as she took the potted plant. "My mother would die of shame if I showed up empty handed. I wanted to get you flowers, but Clara at Greenley's said their regular delivery was delayed and this was all she had in stock. Well, this or two bunches of wilted roses and I thought giving you those would be worse than this."

"It's fine. The dining room table is still huge and empty, so this will fill the room." Even without the tradition attached to it, the poinsettia was a breathtaking display. The flowers practically shone under the dining room chandelier and were a bright white rather than a muted cream. It elevated the whole room, centred on the bare wood table.

She nudged it into position, and jumped back when she heard a crash in the other room. "Oof! Sorry, Jilly," Ben called.

She hurried back to the living room and found him balancing on one foot while glaring at a flat, square box that was now in the middle of the floor. "What happened?" she asked.

"I cut the corner too closely and kicked this box. What's in it, a brick?"

"A wreath for the door. Dan gave it to me, but I haven't put it up."

"I can do it right now," he offered.

"That's not necessary."

"It'll get it off the floor and open up more space in your living room. If you trip over it and land on your other arm, you'll be in real trouble."

That was true. It was doing nothing in the house but taking up space, and the wreath wasn't something she could keep till next year. It was already a little dried out from being in the house for two weeks, although the boughs still held their green. "I don't have a hanger for the front door."

"I heard something metal when I kicked it. There might be one in the box."

She opened the cardboard flaps, and Ben lifted the wreath. Sure enough, a metal door hanger tumbled from the boughs and landed in the bottom of the box. "I'll hang this on the front door while you break down the box," Ben offered.

"You can hang it, but I'm keeping the box. It's a good one." She had a policy of never letting a good box go to waste. "I'll put it in the spare room closet to get it out of the way," Jilly compromised.

It only took a minute for the wreath to go up. She didn't go outside to check it out though. She trusted Ben got it straight. "Now for supper."

"What kinds did you get?" Ben asked, eying the still-hidden pizza tops.

"Pepperoni, mushroom and green pepper. And a surprise."

He eyed her suspiciously. "Surprises on a pizza are never good. What is it? Anchovies?"

"Ack! No way."

He turned up his nose. "Pineapple?"

"There's nothing wrong with pineapple on pizza, but no."

"Then what?"

Jilly grinned. "I ordered it special for you. Half is a meat-lover's deluxe. The other half..." She reached for the lid. "Wait. I'll show you." She folded the cardboard back triumphantly and watched Ben's eyes open wide.

"What is that?"

"Roasted Brussel sprouts, roasted garlic, and bacon."

Now they were even for the cinnamon buns.

She burst into laughter and he shrugged. "I'll give it a try. But you'll have to have a slice as well."

"Fair enough."

It was surprisingly good, but Jilly believed the wine and company had a lot to do with it. Although they both said they enjoyed the new concoction, they both moved on to the other flavours after the first piece.

She could have eaten another slice, but the bakery box on the kitchen counter called her name. "What did you get from Totally Iced? How did you get something from Totally Iced? Kris Singleton doesn't do out-of-province shipments this late in the year." Jilly would know; every year, she tried to sneak one past the Alberta bakery, but she always got caught.

"I had a friend doing a run to Calgary. These were the

hot sellers the day he was able to ask Rudy to grab something for him and hand it over at the warehouse."

The mini loaf of dark fruitcake inside upheld the reputation. "I don't need another glass of wine after that. Hello, rum!"

"If I have another slice, I'll be walking home."

She snorted. Like he'd be getting any leftovers.

Since they were both stuffed full of good food, warm inside in front of the fire, and relaxing with their wine, Jilly figured a better opportunity would never present itself.

"I need to apologize to you," she said. Jilly hated this part, but it was necessary. "For snapping at you after my conversation with Joy about the cat. My aversion to Christmas this year is my own problem, and I'm sorry I took it out on you to the point where you're afraid to say the word."

"You're allowed to have your feelings."

"I know, but these were stupid feelings. I'm getting Ben and Alex on the twenty-sixth, so even if I open the gift my parents left me on the twenty-fifth when I'm by myself, I still get another whole day of presents and food and family and celebrations. I should be excited about doubling my Christmases, not mourning one I never really lost."

Ben toasted her with his wineglass. "You don't need to apologize. I knew you'd get here in the end. Here's to all the Christmases this year, no matter when they're celebrated."

She drank, then asked, "Did you have other plans on Christmas Eve? I'm sure you want to see your mom. I didn't mean to put you on the spot when I asked Eve if you could come." But she really wanted him to.

He hand-waved her concern. "I've got breakfast plans with my mom, and a video call scheduled with cousins, but I'm free for most of the day. I'd love to be your Christmas Eve date."

Jilly's sigh of relief went down to her toes. "Thank you. Now all I have to do is apologize to Joy for jumping down her throat."

"Are you going to take the cat?"

"No. Not this time. I feel like I need more time to work up to that. I lost Buster a couple years ago but I'm still not ready. But now the idea's in my head, I might be open to the next litter. I owe her something though. I'm thinking of—"

"Canned salmon?" Ben interrupted.

"Yeah. Great minds think alike. Maybe a twelve-pack of salmon for the cats she's taking care of, with extra ribbons to keep the cats and kittens occupied," Jilly said.

"I'm sure she'd appreciate it."

"Now all I have to do is buy the ingredients for a huge batch of my hot chocolate to take to Helen's, and I'll be all set."

She didn't understand why Ben laughed.

Jilly didn't want to say the evening was going too well to last because she was trying as hard as she could to hold on to her Christmas spirit. But when her house phone rang, her heart sank. Nobody would be calling at this hour with good news. "Hello?" she said into the receiver.

"Hi, Mom."

"Dan! What's up?" She heard him take a breath before speaking and knew her fears were justified. "Dan, what's wrong?"

"Alex just got a call from his best friend. He's getting married over the holidays and wants Alex to be the best man. The whole wedding is spur of the moment. They think they can pull it all together in a week."

Jilly held the receiver away from her face so her son wouldn't hear her sigh. She knew where this was going. "Where?"

"Up in Dauphin."

"When?"

Dan hesitated again. "On Boxing Day. In the afternoon."

"So you won't be able to come home until the twenty-seventh?"

"I'm so sorry, Mom. It was a last-minute decision, and they've been friends since grade school. I can send my apologies and still leave first thing in the morning. Alex and I can take separate cars, and he can drive down the next day," he offered.

Suddenly, the fireplace wasn't putting off enough heat, and the glow of the fake candles was swallowed by the evening darkness. Even Ben seemed further away, although he hadn't moved from his spot on the sofa.

"Or you could go to Alex's best friend's wedding and have a good time and celebrate with them," Jilly countered, keeping her voice as firm as she could. She locked her body rigid, holding back the urge to yell, "No, come home and spend the day with your mother!" even though that's all she wanted to say.

"Mom..."

"What I said before stands," she insisted. It was true: Christmas wasn't a day on the calendar. It could also be the day you chose to celebrate it with friends and family. One more day late wouldn't take away the laughter in Dan's eyes when he opened the geeky T-shirt Santa was leaving for him under the tree, or dim the smile Alex would give her when he unwrapped the framed photo of him and Dan after they'd crossed the finish line at the charity mud run they'd done the previous spring. It was only one more day. "We can have Christmas on the twenty-seventh as easily as the twenty-sixth. You should celebrate with Alex and his friends, and not begrudge them their wedding date."

"Are you sure?"

Her son was *such* a good kid. "I'm positive. Wish the happy couple congratulations for me. I'll see the both of you on the twenty-seventh. Call me on Christmas morning, okay?"

"I will. I love you, Mom."

Ben was beside her when she hung up the phone. "What happened? Is Dan not coming home for Christmas?"

"No. Something came up and they're going to be late." He wrapped an arm around her shoulder, and she didn't resist when he pulled her closer. Jilly let her head drop against his chest. "What matters is that he's still coming on the twenty-seventh, right?" she said, her voice muffled by his shirt.

"Right," he agreed.

"It's wonderful that he has someone special." Otherwise he'd end up alone and bitter at Christmas like her.

"It is."

"Celebrating a friend's wedding is a wonderful way to end the year."

"Wonderful."

Jilly released the sigh she hadn't let Dan hear. "This sucks donkey balls."

"It does." She smiled briefly when he hugged her harder.

She shouldn't let this ruin her holiday. She'd worked hard to get out of her funk. What was an extra twenty-four hours in the big scheme of things? She could find something to do on Boxing Day. Online shopping. A movie marathon. Maybe Ben was free.

It wouldn't be easy to keep hold of her cheer, but she'd do her best.

CHAPTER 15

CHRISTMAS EVE BREAKFAST with family was a thing at the Sunset Retirement Residence. It was an open breakfast for all the residents and their families, which allowed them all to get together, in case Christmas Day dinner wasn't an option. His mom and the other residents contributed to the community potluck, with tons of pastries, loaves, and fruit plates.

Ben laughed when he saw Mr. Wojowitz and Mrs. Johnson appear in costume. By design, the residents received their presents from Jilly's Gifts for Seniors group on Christmas Eve, and left the decision of when to open them to the recipients. He saw a few piles of torn wrapping paper and some items he recognized, but most of the people seemed content to hold on to them for later.

He, on the other hand, would have opened it immediately. He always felt an unopened present was a waste. Which explained why his mother said she wasn't handing his over until the next day.

"Thank you for coming to brunch today," she said.

"Of course, Mom. It's really hopping in here." The

same community room where they'd held the auditions was again packed, this time with people of all ages, and ten times the noise. "I'm glad you invited me."

"I wanted to introduce you to some new friends who aren't going to be here later." She waved at someone behind him, and Ben rose to his feet, expecting one of the bridge partners she'd talked about.

He was not expecting a white-haired man, with slightly hunched shoulders, and a bushy mustache. "Hello, Ebenezer. I'm Marlon Timchuk. It's nice to meet you. Belle talks about you all the time."

His mother had a gentleman friend. Ben didn't know what to do with that. Fortunately, good manners had been ingrained since birth, so his handshake and returned greeting were automatic. "Ben, please. I'm happy to meet you too. Mom has told me nothing about you, but won't you join us for some cake and coffee?"

His mother had a gentleman friend. It had been a decade since his father passed away, and she hadn't shown any interest in dating. She'd been in the Sunset for a matter of months and had found a new group of friends and a man who made her smile. Ben looked at her face. Beam, he corrected, watching the two of them chat about their friends who'd received gifts that day.

"No, thank you. My daughter and her husband are driving out today from Winnipeg. I'll be staying with them and my grandkids for a few days. Belle says you'll be coming to see her tomorrow."

"Yes, he's not getting any presents till then. He'll open them as soon as he sees them. We were the only family on the block who didn't put presents under the tree before Christmas," his mother teased.

"What can I say? I like my presents, and I want them as soon as I see them," Ben said.

Marlon moved on to a new group soon after, staying only long enough to introduce himself and have a little chat. "Well, that was exciting," Ben said in a deadpan voice after he left.

"Do you mind?"

"Not at all, Mom. I'm surprised, not mad. I think it's great you're meeting new people. You never would have had a chance to if you were still in the house." Not *home*. Now she had him doing it.

"That's what I've been telling you. Dr. Francis even said my blood pressure, mental acuity, and physical fitness are all showing signs of improvement since I moved in. Not to mention my love life."

Ben threw up his hands. "No comments on your love life! I'm glad you have one, but I don't need to know the details!"

"Then can we talk about yours? Are you spending any of the holidays with Jilly?" Her brown eyes, identical to his, sparkled with interest.

"I'm taking her to a Christmas Eve open house this afternoon. Then she'll be on her own tomorrow, and her son and his boyfriend are coming home the day after Boxing Day."

"The Klassen open house?"

"No, that's on the twenty-fifth. This is just some friends."

"I hope you have a wonderful time with her. Did you get her a gift?"

"Yes, but I'm not sure when I'll give it to her. Maybe I'll stop over tomorrow, so she'll have a present on Christmas Day," he said. He didn't want Jilly to spend the day alone, especially since her son wasn't coming home until two days after that.

"That sounds lovely." His mother slowly stood, then bent over to give him a hug while he was seated so she could reach his shoulders. "Thank you for coming to our breakfast. I'll see you tomorrow. I love you, Ebenezer."

"I love you too, Mom."

He had enough time to walk Sprite, play with her, have lunch, and walk the puppy again before he left to pick up Jilly. Ben had hauled all kinds of things over the years—large, small, frozen, alive—but his biggest challenge was transporting a half-full crockpot of hot chocolate across town without spilling it all over his floor mats.

"Maybe I should have added the marshmallows early to give it a kind of cover," Jilly fretted.

"You said they'd dissolve too early if you did that."

"Then slow down and stop aiming for the potholes!"

He tapped the breaks and dropped from a creep to a crawl for the last two blocks. Eve's tow-truck was parked in the street, and Clementine was right behind it. They had to park two doors up. Jilly slung a bag with containers of cookies over her shoulder and waited for Ben to follow with the Crockpot.

Helen Gauthier's house was lit in every room, even at three o'clock in the afternoon. Her teenaged daughter, Emily, met them at the door and whisked away the Crockpot to the kitchen to pluck it in. Eve took their coats, and they walked into the living room as a kid in a bunny suit walked down the stairs on the television.

"Welcome to the party. We have a buffet-type snack bar on the living room table, and hot food will be coming out at five o'clock. The bar is in the kitchen, and we're starting a puzzle on the coffee table. Feel free to join in anywhere," Helen said.

Nick was noshing on a plate of pumpernickel pieces and spinach dip. Emily waited for them to take their seats on the sofa, and then dropped cross-legged in front of the coffee table and picked up a box of puzzle pieces. "I'm looking for the other corner piece and the edges to get the frame done," she told him.

"What's the picture?" Jilly asked. "I'll help."

Emily handed over a lid, which showed a picture of Van Gogh's "Starry Night."

"Oh, very nice!" She stuck her hand in the box and pulled out a piece with a flat side. "Edge piece!" she crowed triumphantly.

Ben relaxed into the cushions and enjoyed looking around the room. A real spruce tree stood at a slight lean in the corner, decorated with so many strings of lights it looked white, colour-coordinated balls of light and dark blue, and strands of silver tinsel, which Ben hadn't seen since the eighties, decorated the branches. Three red stockings hung from the gas fireplace mantle, two regular-sized, and one that stretched all the way to the floor. A string of clothespins holding Christmas cards hung above the front window. The Gauthiers and LeBlancs seemed to have Christmas well under control.

With a plate of goodies and a cup of cheer, Ben took a seat beside Nick. The other man had a laptop set up on a small table and was playing The Best and Worst Plays of the Year on a sports website. It beat the ending of the movie the women were watching. As soon as the credits started to roll, Emily got up to switch DVDs. She started a new one, then disappeared to the kitchen.

"This is nice," Ben said.

"The ladies do a really cozy Christmas Eve. It's much more laid-back than my family's open house tomorrow," Nick said. "What are you doing tomorrow?"

Ben shrugged. "I'm not sure. I'm having supper and a visit with my mom, but aside from that, it might be me and Sprite."

"What about Jilly?" The question came from Emily, who'd returned through a different doorway holding a plate of cookies and a lone carrot stick.

"I think she'll be taking it easy. Daniel was supposed to come home on the twenty-sixth, but it got pushed back a day."

Emily frowned. "Oh, no. He said she wasn't handling his first Christmas away from home very well." When she noticed his look, she shrugged. "We go to university together. My last exam was three days before his, so I've been home for a while. He asked me to check on her. I'm glad I'll be able to tell him she came over today."

A burst of laughter drew their attention to Helen, Eve, and Jilly, who were pointing at the screen.

"With hair," Jilly insisted.

"Bald," Helen argued. "Bruce Willis is much sexier bald. Eve, you have to break the tie."

"Alan Rickman," Eve said.

They went silent. "I can live with that," both women agreed.

He and Nick shared a look and decided to ignore that whole exchange. "Tell Daniel she had a very good time," Ben said.

"Will do."

Ben noticed a puzzle piece fall off the table when Emily set down her plate. He crossed the room to pick it up, and when he bent over to put it back onto the table, he spotted where it went, so he pressed it into place instead. Then he saw where another place went. Before he knew it, Jilly had slid over and he was sitting beside her, racing to see how many pieces they could fit.

Before long, the credits were rolling on the movie and Helen was carrying large glass pie plates to the dining room table. The spicy scent of meat pie drifted into the living room. He and Jilly guiltily checked the time on their phones.

"Oh, my. We never expected to stay so long. I'm sorry, Helen, we'll get out of here so you can have supper."

"You're not staying?"

"We won't impose."

Helen put her hands on her hips. "Let me rephrase. Why aren't you staying? I have three large tourtieres, a gallon of gravy, and vegetables for days. I planned on pawning at least a third of a pie off on you, preferably half, if Ben will take thirds. What are you going to do, go home and throw a frozen dinner in the microwave?"

"Not anymore?" Jilly replied hesitantly.

"Good answer. If one of you want to bring out the stack of plates from the kitchen, the other can bring out the silverware. If you'd like to help."

"Of course, we'll help." Ben's mother hadn't raised a fool. They got dished up just before there was a knock on the door. Joy and Decker Harkness stood on the front step, bearing a wine bottle.

"Yay, we're in time for dinner!" Decker said.

"Come and get it while it's hot."

Ben thought the living room would be too crowded for everyone to have a seat, but Eve got a call while the other couple were loading their plates. "It never fails," Eve said. "Every year somebody ends up in a ditch. They sound fine, but I'll be gone for at least a couple hours" She pulled him and Jilly into hugs. "Thanks for coming over today. I had a good time doing the puzzle with you."

"Thanks for the invitation," Jilly said.

The beef and pork pie was as delicious as it smelled, and the new guests kept the conversation jumping with talk of animal antics and their upcoming Valentine's ski trip to Whistler. Joy was especially excited about a tour of a local flower shop Decker had promised her.

As soon as they were finished, Ben took a look at Jilly and realized her engaged smile was faltering as talk turned to family plans. "Helen and Emily, thank you very much for a great afternoon and a wonderful supper. We'll leave you to your other guests."

"Yes, thank you very much. Have a wonderful Christmas," Jilly said.

She was quiet on the drive back to her house. "Are you okay?" he asked.

"Better than okay. This afternoon was exactly what I needed. A low-key Christmas Eve. It was enough to get me out of the house and in the mood to do some preparations for Danny and Alex. Maybe I'll make a batch of cookies tomorrow."

"That sounds more like the Jilly I know and lo—like," Ben said. "I'm glad you found your Christmas spirit.

"It's a little dented from being under a pile of coal, but I'll dust it off by the time Danny gets home."

Brightly lit houses guided their way home. "What about you?" Jilly asked. "What are you doing tomorrow?"

"I'm visiting my mom and spending some time with Sprite. It's supposed to be relatively nice, so maybe we'll have some playtime in the park."

"You should come over," she said. "All of you. We

won't have a dinner, but since you're having one at the Sunset later, maybe you'd like to have a light lunch at my place. Sandwiches or something?"

"That sounds great. I'll ask my mom, but Sprite and I will be over for sure. Is your house puppy-proof?"

"It will be by tomorrow." Her voice sounded buoyed by the prospect of company, especially of the four-footed variety. "It'll be quiet, but fun."

"And I'll have a chance to give you your present," Ben added.

"You got me a present?"

Was she kidding? He'd been piecing together her gift since he'd decided to quit driving. "We're dating, aren't we?"

"Then you can have yours tomorrow too." A horrified look crossed her face. "Oh, no! I forgot my crockpot at Helen's house. All that cocoa, and I only saw a couple people have some."

"Give her a call when you get home and tell her to make sure whoever comes over this evening gets a mugful. Eve will probably want something warm when she gets back. I can pick it up and bring it back to you tomorrow," Ben promised. He had no doubt the basin would be empty and scrubbed by the end of the night.

"I'll make fresh stuff for you and your mother."

"You don't have to."

"I want to."

"Then hot chocolate we will have."

Anything to keep Jilly smiling.

CHAPTER 16

JILLY SAW the clock hit midnight on Christmas Eve, and greeted the wee hours of Christmas morning with Jimmy Stewart, Maureen O'Hara and Alastair Sim. She finished the wine from her at-home supper date with Ben from earlier in the week and polished off seven chocolate covered shortcake cookies from Totally Iced, but she resisted opening the last box she was saving for Daniel's visit. Then she stumbled to bed and spent the remainder of the night enjoying sugarplum dreams.

With her electric blanket on, she floated to consciousness feeling toasty warm, wondering what woke her to the sun shining through her bedroom window. Then she heard a thump. Followed by a deep male voice shouting, "Ho, ho, ho!"

Jilly went from half-asleep to standing on her bed, brandishing the book from her bedside table as a weapon in a blink.

The voice called out again. "Mom?"

It took a minute to get her heart out of her throat and beating again. "Danny? I'm still in bed. One second and

I'll be right down." Jilly grabbed the fuzzy blue robe hanging on the back of her closet door and raced to the front door, fumbling with the thick belt as she tried to tie it shut over her plaid, flannel pajamas. "Danny? What are you doing here? I didn't sleep through till the twenty-seventh, did I?" She'd had a good night's rest but that was ridiculous.

Her son stood in the doorway, shucking his jacket and toeing off his boots, with an even taller young man behind him doing the same. "Merry Christmas morning, Mom!"

Jilly didn't bother to ask any questions. She gave Daniel a big hug, and then pulled in Alex. "What on earth are you doing here? You weren't supposed to arrive until the day after tomorrow."

The tall redhead behind Dan threw up his hands. "My family's Christmas Eve tradition of baked salmon did not go over well this year. Everyone who ate it was up all night with food poisoning. Our Christmas supper has been postponed till tomorrow night." Alex looked embarrassed.

"What about your best man duties?" Jilly asked as she ushered them into the kitchen and started the coffee maker.

"The spur of the moment wedding hit a snag. Their flight to Mexico got bumped up to six o'clock tomorrow morning, so they're having their honeymoon first and doing the ceremony when they get home. Danny said you wouldn't mind if we showed up today. Do you?"

"Of course not. I'm sorry to hear about your family and hope they are all recovering, but I'm thrilled you're here!" She hugged them both again. Jilly couldn't believe Santa had given her the one thing she really wanted for

Christmas. She'd have to outdo herself on next year's float.

Her mind whirled. "Since it was just the three of us, I was planning on a cooking a little chicken instead of a big turkey, but it's not defrosted. We can drop it in the sink and eat a little later. I have most of the ingredients for the side dishes, but none of them are prepared. And—"

"Mom! Let's start with you getting showered and dressed, and I'll finish making the coffee," Daniel interrupted with a laugh.

"Right. Lots of coffee," she pleaded. Jilly made it to her bedroom before she retraced her steps. "I invited Ben and his mother over for a Christmas lunch at noon."

"Then shouldn't you get dressed?"

"Why?"

"Because it's already after ten," Daniel said.

"What?" The clock on the stove said he wasn't lying. "I'm not ready!"

"Mom, go shower. Alex and I will take care of it."

Jilly thought she set new speed records getting ready, but— "How long was I gone?"

"What?" Daniel asked.

She waved her hand around. "All of this." It looked like St. Nick had snuck in through the chimney while she was sleeping and decorated her entire house, including the boys.

She hadn't noticed that Dan was wearing his brown reindeer sweater with the red pompom nose sticking out in the middle of his chest. Alex wore a button-down white shirt with a blue snowman tie. But their clothes were barely noticeable compared to everything else.

"All the dishes were in the dishwasher, and I couldn't wash them by hand while you were in the shower. Then I saw your Christmas china bin in the dining room. I figured you intended to use them for your lunch, so I set the table with them. While I did that, I told Alex how to assemble your wire ornament stand and showed him your box of antique ornaments. We put that up in the living room. Then we stacked the empty bins in the spare room to get them out of the way," Daniel explained. "I was worried when Emily told me Mrs. Gauthier said you weren't decorating this year, but when we got here the exterior Christmas lights were on and the wreath was on the door."

"The mantle looks pretty with the candles and photos. My mom does the same thing," Alex added.

"We figured you'd been working too hard on the Santa float to get around to finishing since the rest of the boxes were still out," Daniel finished. "It was no problem."

That glowing report from her son, and his obvious relief that she'd been willing to celebrate Christmas without him, made her want to tear up. "Thank you. You are both very efficient elves," was all she could say.

Jilly was still reeling from the decoration blitz when the doorbell rang. "They can't be here. It's not even eleven thirty!" She needed to get the soda bread in the oven, and the butternut squash soup out of the freezer and into the pot to defrost and heat. She had to assemble the dainty tray for dessert. She'd never been so thankful for her restraint, since the night before she'd forgotten she needed cookies for lunch and not just for the boys.

"Relax, Mom, it's not them," Daniel said as he motioned for Alex to open the door.

"Who else would be here on Christmas morning?" Jilly demanded.

"Merry Christmas!" Madison Hill preceded her box-laden mother into the house.

"Madison? Amanda?"

"Thank you, Jilly. We appreciate this so much! I was desperate but when Danny said we could use your oven, you became the neighbour who saved Christmas!" Amanda stepped around her and headed straight into the kitchen, where she slid her box onto the counter.

"Danny said what?"

Amanda froze. "Danny said we could use your oven," she repeated slowly.

"Yeah, Ms. Lewis, thanks. My dad is deep frying the turkey in the garage, but Mom needs to make the green bean casserole and the sweet potato pie in the oven and ours went *whoomp* and started smoking when she turned it on this morning," Madison explained. The little girl shook her head sadly, the green ribbons on her short, black pigtails bobbing. "My grandpa loves green bean casserole."

"We can call Eve and see if we can use her place if it's a problem," Amanda said.

"I was in the shower when Danny spoke to you, but of course you're welcome to use an oven. That's the benefit of having double ovens. You use one, I'll use the other, and everyone will get a fantastic Christmas dinner," Jilly said.

"I'm going to draw you a thank-you picture," ten-year-old Madison said.

Jilly smiled at the tiny trooper. The last time Madison had made her a picture, the little girl was thanking her for the new barrettes Jilly gave her when her hair started growing back after her chemotherapy was over. "I'll make a space in the middle of fridge to show it off," she promised.

Amanda had to remove a rack in order to get both dishes into the oven. "These only take an hour, so if I can pop them in now, we'll come back before one."

"Whenever you need. We'll be home all day, and my kitchen is your kitchen. Except the island. I'll need that space."

Amanda laughed. "That sounds more than fair. Thank you."

When the doorbell rang again, Jilly's panic surged a second time. "They can't be here. I'm still not ready. Stall them!" She still had to pull the chicken out of the freezer and get it defrosting in the sink for supper that night, get the big pot for the mashed potatoes out of the pantry, and arrange the boys' presents under the tree.

"Relax, Mom. It's not them."

"Who else would be here on Christmas morning? Besides our dear friends, the Hills, who need to borrow our oven?" After a month of playing the Grinch, Jilly wasn't going to backslide now that she'd finally got her holiday spirit back. But having random people show up on her doorstep on Christmas morning was enough to throw anyone for a loop.

"Jilly, you are a doll. An angel walking the earth," Joy said.

"And modest. Don't forget modest," Jilly teased.

"The most modest, wonderful, generous friend the world has ever seen," Joy agreed.

"Thanks, Joy. Remind me again why I'm so great?" Because she had no idea what was going on. "Danny didn't have time to tell me the full story."

A bustle at the front door had everyone moving further down the hall when Decker appeared holding a large, blanket covered cat carrier. "We woke up at four thirty to a freezing cold house and Pumpkin and the terrible trio burrowing under our covers. The kittens were in their carrier meowing pitifully. I warmed them up with an electric blanket while Decker looked at the furnace. Then he warmed up some milk for all of them while I looked at the furnace. We have an emergency repairman coming out, but we couldn't stay in the house with the cats any longer. Helen and Emily will be gone all afternoon at the Klassen open house, so both of those families are out for kitten-sitting. Clara Dempsey agreed to take the big cats for today since the grocery store is closed, but she couldn't handle the kittens. Dr. Farnsworth already has three, and Dr. Kovac took two. Amanda's not picking up her phone. I wouldn't have asked except—"

"Get in here and take off your coats," Jilly said. Nobody was freezing to death on her watch. "Of course, Daniel said you should come over." As she squeezed by him, she whispered, "Although a little warning would be nice."

She stowed Joy and Decker's coats in the front closet and took the carrier into the living room, setting it in front of her gas fireplace. At that distance, the kittens would receive a little warmth from the flickering flames without getting too hot. "We'll let them out in a little while. You're lucky. I spent last night on my hands and knees looking for things Ben's puppy might chew on, so the living room and dining room should be fine for your little fluffballs to run around in." She'd eradicated a colony of dust bunnies in her quest and had to toss her clothes directly into the laundry hamper as a result, but she was satisfied her house would be safe for Sprite as long as they kept an eye on her. Now she was glad she hadn't put off the task.

"My darling son, did you get that pot of coffee made? I think we can all use some. Except for Madison. She can have some hot chocolate."

"Thank you, Jilly, but we have to get home to make sure the rest of our Christmas dinner is organized. We'll see you in a bit."

The house was slightly less full when the Hills left, but then Decker let the kittens out of the carrier, and confusion reigned. Fortunately, the boys offered to keep them company while Jilly pulled out everything she needed for lunch. Stretching her supplies to cover seven where there was going to be barely enough for three had her in a mad panic.

Then she remembered the deli ham she'd been planning for dinner that night. Now it was lunch. Along with the coleslaw she'd bought with it, a package of butter pan buns, and the ingredients for the salad she'd intended for Boxing Day. If she could throw together a cheese and pickle platter, and get a dainty tray ready, she could fake the rest. All she needed was ten minutes to throw it together.

She didn't get it. The doorbell rang again. This time, the bark on her front step let her know it was the one set of guests she'd actually been expecting.

"Decker and Joy, Ben is bringing Sprite, and I don't know if she's met kittens before," Jilly called in warning.

She didn't expect laughter. "Don't worry, she knows them quite well. We socialized a lot at Penny's place earlier last month," Joy said. "Although I must admit I'm glad you don't have a Christmas tree up. That would have been interesting."

Jilly took a deep breath. This was not the first social event she wanted to have with her boyfriend's mother. She'd planned something quiet and simple and dignified, not with two extra, unexpected sets of guests and a menagerie. But it was what it was, and she refused to close her door to anyone on Christmas Day, especially friends.

"Merry Christmas, Mrs. Fredericks. Hi, Ben." She felt her cheeks burn bright red when he gave her a quick kiss hello in front of his mother.

"Please call me Belle. Is this your son?" the older woman asked.

"My son Daniel and his boyfriend Alex. I wasn't expecting them till the day after tomorrow but luckily, they were able to come home for Christmas. I hope you don't mind the extra company."

"Not at all. How exciting to have your boys home after all!"

Sprite lunged on her leash toward the living room, and Ben almost went with her. "It's a great surprise. Nice to see you again, Dan. Who else is here?"

"Joy and Decker. Their furnace broke and they're staying here until the repairman gets here. Oh, and they brought some furry little friends. Comet, Donder and Blitzen. Joy assures me they'll get along with Sprite."

"Kitten lap warmers. This keeps getting better by the minute," Belle said. "Let's go wish them a merry Christmas."

Jilly's living room was a fair size, but the boys had to bring in dining room chairs and sit with their backs to the bookshelves along the wall to keep the conversation flowing. And it did flow. Tales of Christmases past, and since the four represented families hadn't heard each other's stories before, they had everyone in stitches.

"It's true," Belle insisted. "Ebenezer was devastated on Christmas Eve and wouldn't tell his father or me why. He didn't want to open his presents on Christmas morning. But when we made him, he cried as he opened the first one."

"Why?" Jilly asked.

"It seems he had unwrapped all the packages he found in my closet, and then rewrapped them without us noticing. But what he didn't know was we were holding our neighbour's presents because their daughter was also a snooper. Ebenezer had unwrapped a Barbie and several outfits, a copy of Candyland, and cake mixes for an Easy Bake oven. He thought that's what he was getting for Christmas!" Belle revealed with a howl.

Everyone laughed, even Ben, who tried to hold a frown on his face "It wasn't funny at the time." Then he snickered. "I was never so glad to see Stretch Armstrong in my life!"

When Alex leaned over and asked Jilly, "Who's Stretch Armstrong?" she only laughed harder.

She stood and was about to ask the boys to help her get lunch on the table, when there was another knock on the door. Daniel raised his hands. "This time it's wasn't me."

"It's that lady and her little girl again," Alex said, his position letting him see out the front window to the stairs. "Bearing gifts," he added.

"It can't have been an hour already." But a glance at the grandfather clock in the corner confirmed that it was already half past noon. The Christmas Day she'd been dreading was flying by much too quickly.

Jilly excused herself and took Amanda and Madison to the kitchen. Madison handed over a ceramic pie plate piled with berry-filled squares. "They are cranberry and blueberry breakfast cake," Madison said. "Mom and I made them yesterday before the oven exploded."

"We figured you could use something extra to help with your unexpected guests," Amanda added. Then she pulled a tube of crescent rolls out of her shopping bag. "We're also hoping to impose on you for another twenty minutes."

That was something Jilly had in her refrigerator as well. "Only if you put my tray in with yours."

Madison rolled, Amanda shuffled things around in the oven, and Jilly began carving the ham. When Joy wandered in a moment later asking if she could help, Jilly told her to wash her hands and start slicing pickles. Daniel came in to start a new pot of coffee. Alex came looking for Daniel, then ignored him as he exchanged tips with Amanda about how to keep the proper consistency in a green bean casserole. Daniel started sneaking Madison cookies while the grown-ups talked around her. Then Decker came in to inform Joy that the kittens had crashed and were all sleeping in their carrier, and hot on his heels were Belle, Ben, and Sprite, who wanted to know where everyone went. Belle took over the pickle board after they set her up with a stool at the island, and Joy moved onto cutting cheese blocks into smaller cubes.

The kitchen was a zoo, with barely enough room if a person wanted to turn around. The three different conversations happening at the same time filled it with noise. It smelled of cranberries and cinnamon and pie.

It was perfect.

Jilly wiggled around the island until she was side by

side with Ben. She slipped her arm around his waist and leaned close to his ear. "Did you do this?" she asked quietly.

"Do what?"

"Bring me Christmas." A house full of people, a heart full of happiness, and a day full of memories about to be made.

"I wish I could take credit, but all this happened on its own, and because of you."

Jilly snuggled closer when his arm wrapped around her. "I'm glad you're part of it."

"I wouldn't have missed it for the world. I love seeing you at Christmas time. In fact, I love..."

The statement she was hoping he'd make was cut off by a purr and a howl and then an explosion of fur and laughter, as the supposedly locked-up kittens wandered into the kitchen and Sprite pounced at them playfully. Joy dove for the kittens, while Daniel and Alex went for the puppy.

The moment was gone, but Jilly still had time to say, "Me too."

"Merry Christmas, Jilly."

EPILOGUE

THE FLAMES FLICKERED over the logs in the fireplace. Jilly set her wine glasses on the table and then fell into a mound of pillows on the sofa. Ben lifted a fluffy throw blanket from her reading chair and draped it over her legs. "Today was intense," he said. For a woman who wasn't expecting anything more for Christmas than two people for a light lunch, she'd had a full house all day.

The Hills loaded up their casseroles and crescent rolls and departed before the rest of them sat down for a last-minute but thoroughly tasty Christmas luncheon. Decker and Joy had stayed for lunch, then left the kittens behind when the furnace repairman arrived at their house. They returned an hour later to pick up the cats and to thank Jilly for her hospitality. Ben and his mother had departed a little after that, leaving Jilly, Daniel, and Alex to have a family Christmas supper.

At eight o'clock, Jilly had called him to ask how his dinner went. She laughed when he described the ice cream scoop of mashed potatoes and gravy that coved it like chocolate syrup. "It was fine. My mom was grateful we were together for her first Christmas at the Sunset. It had a few hard moments, but we got through them. How was your chicken? And why is it so quiet?"

"Daniel and Alex left right after supper. We opened presents after lunch, then ate again. They decided to head back to Alex's family's place tonight. They'll call when they arrive. That way they can do Christmas again with them, from the stockings forward. They promised to come back again before New Year's Eve."

"I'm sorry they couldn't stay." He'd enjoyed the young men's company and had delighted in the stories Daniel had about his mom. Apparently, roller coaster enthusiasm ran in the family. But, hopefully, there would be other Christmases.

"Me, too, but having them even for a few hours today made my whole holiday. I'm about to crash for the evening on the sofa with a glass of wine and the fire and some quiet. And some company, if you want to come over," she said.

Twenty minutes later he was sitting on the sofa beside her. "Those are some pretty funky slippers, Jilly." He pointed at her feet which were sticking out past her blanket. Blocks of different colours of fake fur made it look like her feet were being swallowed by patchwork Muppets.

"Thanks. Daniel gave them to me."

That's when Ben remembered what had been scratching at his mind all day. "I forgot to give you your present when I was here earlier." He reached under the end table in the corner, and drew out a loosely wrapped, triangular package. "Merry Christmas, Jilly."

He loved that she didn't even pretend to be cool about it. Bows and ribbons flew in all directions until she was left with a unique bouquet in her hands. "Look at this. It's perfect. How did you know?"

"I spoke to your friends." He thought he hit everyone in her knitting group to come up with the perfect assortment of knitting needle "stems" and "flowers" of skeins of yarn wound in balls. He was assured she'd be good for supplies for at least two months, which would take her to Valentine's Day.

"And it's perfect timing. I needed a yarn restock. Thank you." She tossed the blanket aside and pulled a gift-wrapped box out from under the sofa. "For you."

Ben immediately donned the gold toque with a wide royal blue stripe, and a matching scarf. "I match Sprite," he said.

"I know. I planned it that way," she told him.

It was a nice way to end Christmas, Ben thought, the two of them and a quiet glass of wine. Despite the fact they'd been friends for over a year, the last few weeks had shown him they were compatible on a much deeper level.

He hung his arm over the back of the sofa and leaned toward her, and she snuggled into him without hesitation. "What do you think, Jilly?"

Proving they were on the same wavelength, she said, "I think we'll work out fine. We came through our first trial by fire Christmas with no problems. I think that's a good sign going forward."

"You know, I'm fifty. I'm pretty set in my ways at this point." He didn't think either of them thought it would be clear sailing all the time. The more time they spent together, the more differences they would find. But Ben didn't think it would be an insurmountable hurdle either. They could each fold their towels the way they wanted, so

it wasn't like one person would be doing all the compro-
mising on the way things used to be.

"I'm right behind you, and on the plus side, we're both
used to taking care of ourselves, so the things we disagree
on will only be a matter of negotiation and not a fight,"
Jilly said in agreement. "I'm not concerned. Are you?"

"Only that you don't know how crazy I am about you.
I know it seems quick, but I want you to know I love you,
Jilly."

She tilted her head and kissed him on the lips. "I love
you too, Ben."

It was the best Christmas present he'd ever received.

"Now that we've settled that point, do you know
what's next?" Jilly asked.

Her voice held an edge of laughter, and he couldn't
wait to hear what she had to say. "No, what?"

"Planning next year's Christmas float. You just volun-
teered to be my assistant."

"Of course. It's going to be Merry Christmas all year
round with you, isn't it?"

"You know it."

THE END

BONUS RECIPE: CANDY CANE COOKIES

These cookies taste like a peppermint dream. Making them is a ... less pleasant dream. Unlike recipes from my other books, DO NOT MAKE THESE WITH CHILDREN. As a grown-up, I get exasperated trying to roll and shape the delicate cookie dough. With kids, it will be an exercise in frustration. But I promise you they are worth every single fiddly minute.

- I cup butter or margarine, softened
- I cup icing (confectioner's) sugar
- I egg
- I tsp vanilla flavoring
- 2½ cups all-purpose flour
- I tsp baking powder
- I tsp salt
- I tsp almond flavoring
- ¼ tsp peppermint flavoring
- ½ tsp red food coloring

Mix first 4 ingredients together well. Add flour, baking powder and salt. Mix well.

Divide dough into two equal portions. To one half, add almond flavoring. To the other half, add the peppermint flavoring and food coloring. Refrigerate for at least 2 hours. DO NOT SKIP THIS STEP.

Roll 1 tsp of each color dough into ropes about 5-6 inches long. Lay side by side. Pinch ends together. Twist to form a spiral. Keep dough and rolling surface cool. (You may want to keep half the dough in the fridge until you are ready for it.) Place on ungreased cookie sheet and shape to form a cane.

Bake at 350F for about 10 minutes until pale gold.

Cool on baking sheet 2-3 minutes then remove. (Transfer with care; these cookies are delicate.)

Makes about 2 to 3 dozen, depending on how big you make them.

FRANK AND GINGER

A North Pole Unlimited Romance
By
Elle Rush

BLURB

Three weeks until Christmas...

Back in the spring, when Ginger Malone asked charming inventor Frank Cardinal on a date, she struck out hard. Now, at their last business meeting of the year, something has changed, but Ginger won't ask Frank if he's flirting with her in case she's misreading the signs again.

Two hearts afraid to take a chance... Caught flat-footed and tongue-tied when the gorgeous North Pole Unlimited representative asked him out, Frank panicked, and Ginger retreated. Now he's trying to get back to a place where he could have another shot with her, but he might be too late.

One elf-size matchmaker... Grown-ups are so dense! Since her dad hasn't got around to asking Ginger on a date, nine-year-old Michelle is forced to take action with a little help from her friends. Will her risky plan work?

Only Santa knows.

PROLOGUE

"As the last item on today's agenda, Jilly would like a word," Nick Klassen announced to the boardroom full of department heads and other assorted North Pole Unlimited staff. With less than a month until Christmas, they were meeting twice weekly to ensure the company kept on schedule. The good news was everything was winding to a close for their busiest month of the year; the bad news was there was still time for things to go wrong.

Jilly's presentation would give everyone the boost they needed to make it through to the end of the year.

His executive assistant picked up a small, festive bag and began circling the table. "I have a much-desired reward for one individual in attendance today. This person has set the gold standard for the rest of you to follow. For the past eleven months, they have submitted their department's timesheets on time, kept me abreast of changes to vacation schedules, and even handled two transfers out of province and an early maternity leave—all in the same pay period. Their hard work has made my life easier, which, as you all know, should be the goal of everyone here." The room burst into laughter. "I would like to present this small, but highly sought-after gift, to Ginger Malone!"

The redhead at the end of the table stood and took a bow, then carefully set the foil bag in front of her. She gently poked it with the tip of her pencil.

"It's not going to bite. In fact, it's the opposite," Jilly said.

Ginger looked up at her and poked it again. "Are you sure? Chapter five of the North Pole Unlimited Handbook specifically says *beware of Jillys bearing gifts*."

Nick snorted. He tried to turn it into a cough but knew he'd failed when his assistant glared at him. He'd pay for that later, but it didn't mean the comment wasn't deserved. Jilly did have a well-deserved reputation.

"If you don't want it..." Jilly threatened.

Ginger snatched at the gift bag before Jilly could take it back. "I'm opening it!" She removed the tuft of tissue paper and pulled out a tiny food container. She peeled back the lid and gave an excited squeak. "Is this what I think it is?"

"Yes. That, my friend, is a Totally Iced chocolate meringue. You've earned it."

Ginger closed her eyes and raised the cookie to her mouth. "This tastes even better than you said it would," she mumbled, brushing crumbs from her lips.

"I can't believe she got a cookie, and I didn't. I'm your boss," Nick whispered to Jilly.

"Your paperwork was late."

The meeting broke up on that laugh. Ginger gathered her notes and stopped beside Nick and Jilly. "Thanks for the treat. I'm glad I got it before I head out tomorrow."

"Kenora, right?" Although Nick had hundreds of direct employees in his office, and North Pole Unlimited had nearly as many contractors, he'd made a point of learning the files of all of them. "Why do you have to see Frank Cardinal two weeks before Christmas?"

"His latest prototype is ready. I've been getting progress reports on it for months. I can't wait to see the finished product. I'm bringing back a copy for our manufacturing plant for next year's catalogue."

Indie-Genius Games were consistently among the company's best sellers. Every year their newest offering made the Hottest Toys of the Season list. "Santa hasn't delivered this season's game yet. How can Frank have a new one designed already?" Nick asked.

Ginger shrugged. "Maybe he was inspired. All I know is that the longer lead-time we have for his games, the more we seem to sell, so I'm off to get a twelve-month head start on next Christmas," Ginger said.

When it came to picking popular children's games, Ginger Malone had an unmatched success rate. Nick didn't know why she felt the need to pick up the prototype herself when she could send a courier, but he wasn't going to argue with her. "Will you be staying in Kenora overnight?"

The red curls that escaped her braid bounced when she shook her head. "No, it'll be an in and out trip."

"You'll be taking a company vehicle. Right?" Nick

made sure it didn't sound like a question. Kenora was a three-hour drive from December, just across the Ontario-Manitoba border. He wanted to be certain Ginger was in a vehicle that could handle the winter roads, especially since making a round trip meant she'd be starting and ending her day in the dark.

She grinned. "Jilly booked me one of the new SUVs with all the gadgets, including heated seats. My personal car is ten years old. The newest thing in it is a CD player. I may have too much fun to stop driving. If I hit Thunder Bay, I'll turn back," she said with a laugh.

"I wouldn't know about gadgets." Nick drove a refurbished 1940s pickup that he'd inherited from his grandfather. He was thankful it had a heater and a radio, but he wouldn't trade it for the world. It had also introduced him to his fiancée, Eve, after one of its many breakdowns.

"I've heard about Clementine. Don't you think it's time she retired? Come join us in the new millennium. It's only twenty-one years old."

"Never! That old girl is going to last forever."

Ginger licked the last of the chocolate crumbs from her fingers. "Your loss. Thanks for the treat, Jilly. I'll have my December paperwork to you as soon as it's done. Now I have incentive to be on time next year, too, if that's the prize." She gathered her notes and the gift bag and waved on her way out of the room.

"Remember your phone!" Nick yelled at her back. When she didn't respond, Nick sighed. "She's not going to remember. If we need her, we'll have to call Frank."

Jilly sidled up to her boss. "He won't mind. Frank and Michelle will be happy for the company. I was worried about him for the first couple years after his wife passed away, but he and his daughter seem to be doing much better now."

Her seemingly innocent words made Nick's blood run cold. Jilly had a tendency to see matchmaking opportunities everywhere. The fact they often worked out was completely beside the point. "Do I need to worry about you planning something with between Frank and Ginger?"

She grasped her chest, like his accusation had hurt her heart. "Me? Absolutely not. I have absolutely no intention of interfering with the two of them."

Nick *almost* believed her.

CHAPTER 1

SECOND FRIDAY OF DECEMBER, *11:00 a.m.*
  Kenora, Ontario

The new SUV had a built-in GPS system which led
Ginger from her house in December, Manitoba, down the
TransCanada Highway, through Whiteshell Provincial
Park, across the Ontario border, and into the wilds of the
land surrounding the sprawling Lake of the Woods. It was
a gorgeous drive any time of year, but she especially liked
it in the winter when the snow glinted like diamonds on
the spruce trees lining the road, highlighting their blue-
green needles. Ginger was glad she was making the drive
on a sunny day so she could fully appreciate the scenery.
She wouldn't be able to avoid driving in the dark on the
way home, since it was so close to the winter solstice, but
if she got all her business done in a couple hours, she'd
have daylight for part of the return trip.

Ginger loved visiting the Cardinals. Of all the game
and toy suppliers she dealt with, Frank was the only one

she visited personally. She could lie and say it was because he was the only one close to her, but that wasn't true. Or he was the only one her age, since they were both in their early thirties, but that wasn't it either. She just liked him best.

Her initial visits had been all business, and it had been nice to put a handsome face to the name on the contracts. It hadn't taken long for Frank's personality to show itself in person. A few meetings later, the first time she'd flirted with him, he hadn't responded either way. Ginger thought she'd been too subtle, so the previous spring, she'd asked straight out if he'd like to go on a non-business lunch date. Frank had shut her down firmly but kindly. On her two trips since then, Ginger had kept things friendly but purely professional.

She wasn't going to push things with someone she worked with. If he wanted a friend to joke around with, that's what she'd be.

Frank Cardinal and his family lived on the north-east side of Kenora by Rabbit Lake. In addition to the house and separate, three-vehicle garage, the property also had a fully functional outbuilding which acted as the workshop and offices for Indie-Genius Games. Ginger pulled into a parking spot in front of the company's sign.

A short, black-haired blur burst out of the workshop. "Ginger, you're finally here! We've been waiting to show you the new game. You took forever," the little girl hopping outside her car said.

"It's a long drive," Ginger said. Michelle Cardinal was a nine-year-old whirlwind, with her dad's eyes and sense of humour. Ginger made a point of stocking up on science puns whenever she came to visit. "It gave me time to remember a joke. How do astronomers organize a party?"

"I don't know. How?"

"They planet."

A low, deep groan erupted from inside the building. "Really, Ginger? We haven't seen you in two months, and that's the joke you bring to us? That was terrible."

Frank Cardinal held the door open. He wore a blue bandana around his forehead, which was dotted with a thin coating of sawdust, which meant he'd been working on a model. His black hair was pulled back with a tie at the base of his neck. "Come in out of the cold," he said.

Michelle wriggled in her boots as she took Ginger's hand and dragged her inside. "Have you played Dad's new game yet?"

"No, but it sounds like fun. We'll have to try it before I pack it up and take it with me." Ginger knew the premise of Catch Me If You Can. The boardgame was a cross between Sorry and Battleship, involving multiple players, dice, and strategy. It sounded like something she'd want to add to her own game collection.

She hung her coat on the rack by the door and jammed her scarf, mitts, and toque in the sleeve so she could find them later. She kept her boots on, since the building had a concrete floor, and followed him into his workshop.

Frank's workshop was a wonderland of tools, half-assembled prototypes, and blueprints littering every flat surface. A million different game pieces waited their turns in mason jars on shelves. He had a small crock of pens, markers, and pencils next to a larger one of assorted rulers. Altogether, it formed a picture of a game-and-puzzle-loving genius. It suited Frank to a T.

Ginger especially loved that he'd given his nine-year-old her own workstation. At the moment, it looked like

Frank's daughter was in the middle of a maze phase, with strips of balsa wood, bottles of white glue, and tweezers in a towering heap. A paint-stained tile lay in one corner. She also had set a red binder prominently in the centre of the desktop, with "Top-Secret" scrawled across it in thick, black marker. Not only did Michelle look like her dad, she acted like him, too. Ginger thought the pair of them were adorable. She smiled at the thought of the imaginative inventor gene being passed down through the Cardinal line.

"Daddy, can I have your phone for a minute?" Michelle asked.

"Sure, sweetie."

The little girl raced out of the room, giggling as soon as it was in her hand, her Top-Secret binder under her other arm. "Is she working on something?" Ginger asked.

"Probably. Nothing school related though. She's already finished all those projects."

"Still no news on local options?" Michelle's teachers had immediately identified her as someone who needed to be in an accelerated program; the little girl was advanced well beyond her classmates. For the last three years, Frank had arranged tutors and special classes, but Michelle had blown through those like tissue paper. She might be the right age for third grade, but she was working on a sixth-grade curriculum. She was scheduled to graduate from elementary school in June, and Frank was tearing his glossy black hair out at the roots trying to figure out what to do after that.

"I checked out the school in Winnipeg. It's everything you said it was, but I hate the idea of having to board her in another province, three hours away from home." Frank sighed. "Of course, the closest option in Ontario would mean boarding her six hours from home, so that's no better."

"That must be a hard decision," she said.

"It is, but I'd do anything for that kid."

"I know." Ginger turned away and studied his worktable. She didn't want him to see the grin on her face. Super smart, great dad, ridiculously handsome—Frank was too perfect for words. "Where are you hiding Catch Me If You Can? You promised me a sneak peek before you boxed it up."

That got his attention. He did a double take at the bare spot in the middle. "Michelle must have moved it." He spun around, trying to spot it on a nearby space. "I've streamlined the pieces since you saw the original version, and I modified the size of the squares. I kept the same board size as most other family games, so it will fit on the shelves with them in the box. The manufacturer shouldn't have any problems."

His face fell as he gave her the details. "Excuse me," Frank said absently. He wandered to an open cabinet and began rifling through the boxes inside. "I have no idea where she might have put it."

"Do you want me to go find Michelle?"

"That would be great. I'm sure she's gone back to the house. My dad is there."

She loved the fact that he was still close to his parents. Parent, she corrected herself. His mother had passed before Michelle was born. Mr. Cardinal—she couldn't call him Paul no matter how often he told her to—still worked at the landscaping company he'd started himself, although now he worked in the office part-time, rather than outdoors in all four seasons. The rest of the time, he kept an eye on Michelle while Frank was working.

Ginger left Frank poking around in a storage unit and backtracked to the entrance to get her coat. But when she tried the door, it was locked. She jiggled the knob. "Frank, I think the doorknob is broken." She twisted the handle again, in case she'd accidentally pushed it in, but it refused to move.

When he walked over and did the exact same thing, she rolled her eyes, but held her tongue. "Where's the back door?" she asked.

He pointed to the far corner, hidden behind a wall made of cardboard boxes and a free-standing white board. "But it's attached to the fire alarm. That will automatically send a signal. Let me call my dad to let us out. It's strange. I've never had problems with the door before."

He slipped his hand into his jeans pocket, and his eyes got wide. "Michelle has my cell phone. Can we use yours?"

Ginger patted her pants pocket and immediately realized the problem. "Nuts!"

"What?"

"I forgot it." At Frank's gasp, she added, "In the car. I did bring it on the drive for safety. I remembered it before I left the city."

"But not your house?" Frank guessed.

She blushed. "Give me some credit for remembering before I pulled out of the driveway." Some days it felt like she spent half her life retracing her steps to retrieve the stupid thing. At her age, it should be surgically attached to her hand, but it wasn't.

"I'm sure it will be fine. You've only left it outside for a few minutes. It's a warm day." At only two degrees below freezing, it was downright balmy. "I guess we'll have to use the land line." Frank stared hard at his workstation. "I don't remember where it is. I thought it was on the corner of my desk."

Ginger watched him lift various piles of paper and move boxes, grumbling louder after each unsuccessful hunt for the phone. Even in a bad mood he was cute. Usually, there was too much banter for her to have time to study his environment. Now, she knew he sorted his game pieces by size, shape, and material, but not by colour, and that he had no less than three small electronic scales that weighed things down to the gram. She admired the organized chaos he created in until she jumped when he let out a surprised "Oh!" from under the table.

"What?"

He crawled out with a cord dangling between his fingers. "I know why I can't find the phone. It's gone."

CHAPTER 2

HE WAS NEVER GOING to get a second shot at asking Ginger on a date if she thought he was an idiot. Who loses a phone that plugs into a wall? Probably the same type of man who panics when a pretty woman gives him a compliment.

He might be a smart man when it came to toy design, but when it came to women, Frank knew teenagers with more game than him. He hadn't even known Ginger had been flirting with him the first time she did it until his father had teased him later over the supper table about him playing hard to get. He'd honestly thought that she'd just liked his new brown shirt.

Even Michelle had groaned when she'd heard that.

The next time—Frank still had nightmares about that conversation. He'd been on the lookout for another compliment because his father told him that Ginger might have pity on him and try again. He'd rehearsed a bunch he could offer in return. Then she'd thrown him a curveball and knocked all his practiced responses out of his head. "Would you like to go out to lunch with me at the Troutman's Pier, now that we're finished with our meeting?" Ginger had asked. She'd been wearing a pretty floral dress, and a lipstick that looked like cinnamon.

"No thanks," he'd said. Because he was an idiot. He would have gone to the moon with Ginger if she'd asked him, but Troutman's Pier had been shut down by the Health Department the previous week. But did he say that? No. He just turned down her offer without offering an explanation or making an alternate suggestion of a place they could eat.

He could still see the shocked look that had flashed across her face, although she hid it immediately. "Okay," Ginger had continued, like she hadn't said anything at all, "I'll grab something at a drive-through on my way home." Then she confirmed some details about his upcoming contract, and he'd nodded along even though he couldn't understand a word she was saying through the thundering noise in his head.

After she left, he'd locked himself in the workshop for the afternoon before he dared face his family. Michelle had been mad for days.

The next time Ginger had come to Kenora—and it had been four months between visits instead of the usual two—she'd arrived in a business suit. She'd still smiled, and her friendly attitude toward Michelle didn't change, but she'd definitely taken a step backward. Frank didn't know how to fix it. He didn't know if he should, because she might have changed her mind.

"It's gone? Like it's deceased? Did it fall off your desk and break?" Her open mouth made her look as shocked as he felt.

"No. It's just gone. Not here. Vanished." He liked the way she pressed her lips together as she puzzled through the situation. They looked like a rosebud, but there was no way he could work that into the conversation without sounding even more socially awkward than normal.

"Could Michelle have taken it for a history project? Relics of the Twentieth Century or something?" Ginger laughed at her own joke.

He laughed too. "I'll find out when I talk to her. I guess we'll have to send my father an email to come out with the key." Frank groaned. "He'll never let me live this down."

"Do you do this often? Lock yourself in the workshop?"

"No. This has never happened before." But of course, the one time it did happen, it would be with her. He hoped she didn't notice his embarrassed blush. "I'll send that email."

But his computer didn't work either.

Ginger joined him at the desk. She ducked down for moment. "I see the connection problem," she said.

He twisted in his chair until their heads were side by side. The cable from the computer and the cable from the wall lay side by side on the floor, with no modem between them to plug into. It couldn't have been kicked loose; the cables had to be manually unscrewed. Someone had deliberately taken it. And the phone.

One disappearance he could buy. Stuff got moved or broken. But not both at the same time, especially since he'd been online all morning until just before Ginger pulled up. This wasn't an accident, or a coincidence.

"We've been set up."

CHAPTER 3

"SET UP? BY WHOM? FOR WHAT?" How had they gone from the doorknob malfunctioning to being set up for something? Ginger split the hair in her ponytail and gave both handfuls a hearty yank, pulling the elastic band snug against her head. Frank might be adorable, but he could also be as frustrating as Jilly's paperwork.

Then, he didn't answer her.

"Frank?"

Whatever was going on, he wasn't happy about it. His nostrils flared as he breathed in and out through his nose without saying a word. "Michelle's been having a few behavioural issues lately," he said slowly. "I think she locked us in here on purpose."

That sounded completely out of character. "Is she mad at me for suggesting schools in Winnipeg? I've never said anything to her." It wasn't her place. In fact, both she and Frank had taken pains to ensure Michelle hadn't been in any position to eavesdrop on their conversations about her.

Ginger admired Frank immensely for raising his

daughter mostly on his own. His wife had passed away soon after Michelle had been born. He and his dad were doing their best to raise an exceptional little girl, and they were doing a great job, as far as she was concerned. He'd never mentioned having problems with Michelle before. "Is it me being here? Would it help if I apologized?"

"Believe me, you have nothing to apologize for. She's trying to get something from me, and this is not the way to do it." Frank stomped to the door and jammed his thumb against a button in a panel Ginger hadn't noticed before. He pressed it again, and a speaker in the ceiling blared to life.

"Hi, Daddy," Michelle said from the other side of the intercom.

He pointed at a security camera hidden in the corner. "Get your little butt back to the workshop with the phone and modem, and fix whatever you did to the door, little miss, or you are losing your internet privileges for a week."

Ginger shivered at his deep, *don't mess around with me* voice.

"I'm sorry, Daddy, I can't let you out until you complete the quest. The first clue is in the game," the little girl said.

"Let me speak to your grandfather."

"He can't come to the office right now."

"Michelle—"

"Look on my desk under the blanket."

Ginger was closer. She peeked under the heavy, multicoloured blanket. "It's Catch Me If You Can! That explains why we couldn't find it."

"Now you have to play. I love you, Daddy. Have fun, Ginger." An electronic click echoed in the large room and the speaker went dead. The light on the camera stayed green, and the lens zoomed in on them.

Ginger held her hand in front of her mouth. "Can she still hear us?" she whispered.

Frank joined her at Michelle's table. "No. Not when we're this far from the intercom." He turned to glare at the camera, but when his eyes met hers again, she saw a host of emotions play across his face. Embarrassment, concern, annoyance. "I'm so very sorry about this. I don't know what's got into her, but I promise we'll be sitting down to discuss it. I can't believe she locked you in here with me."

She hated the look on his face. "It's okay, Frank. Really. In the grand scheme of things, this prank is less than a minor inconvenience. Oh, dear, I'm locked in a room and ordered to play a game I've been dying to play anyway. Life is so unfair." Her fake-whiny tone drew a small smile, so she continued seriously. "Something is obviously bothering her. This is a small price to pay to find out what it is. Besides"—she paused—"I really want to tell everyone at work that I beat you at your own game. Literally."

The box was blank; they still had to decide on packaging. Inside, she found a board, a plastic baggie with a half-dozen player markers, a deck of instruction cards, and two dice. "Who goes first?"

Frank dragged a stool over from his workstation, while Ginger rolled the chair Michelle had at hers to the other side of the table. "Game on," he said.

Ginger had no idea what she'd been thinking, challenging the game's creator to a match. She got creamed for the first half of the game, but she was beginning a slow comeback. It wasn't going to help if Frank kept rolling the way he was. "That's it. Let me see those. There's no way anybody should be able to get that many doubles." She studied the red dice in her hands, and reluctantly offered them back. "Fine."

"Are you insinuating I'd use loaded dice?"

"I'm insinuating that if it isn't the dice, I'm going to have to rub you for luck," she teased.

When he choked on his coffee, she realized what she'd said. Despite her best intentions, even her subconscious wanted to flirt with him. She had to do better and be more professional; her *friend* Frank deserved it.

But something unexpected happened. Frank took her hand in his, bent over, and blew on the dice gently. "See if that helps."

Was he flirting back? Ginger was so shocked she dropped the dice. They bounced on the board, turned over, and landed on double sixes.

"Are you going to move?" he asked.

She didn't want to. She liked how warm his hand was against hers in the cool air. "Oh, right. Where's my piece?" She counted the spaces twice, and it was only one square behind his.

"You get to go again."

"Right." He wasn't smiling at her any differently than he'd been smiling all morning. Maybe it was some kind of joke he thought she knew. Whatever the reason, he wasn't freaking out about her comment, so she would try to forget it, too. She gave the dice a vigorous shake and threw them on the board again. The fact she got double sixes for the second time in a row paled with the realization that, "I won!"

She never won board games. Or raffles or hockey pools. "I won!" She jumped to her feet, and the chair scooted backward on its casters. Ginger waved her arms and shook her hips. "Winner, winner, chicken dinner!" She cha-chaed around the table. "Gin-ger is a win-*ner*, Gin-ger is a win-*ner*. I love this game."

"Way to go, Miss Malone. You won the game. Now we can get out of here."

That took the wind out of her sails.

Her entire job was marketing strategy; she should have played the situation better. If she'd been smarter, she would have stretched out their time together. "I guess we're free to go then. I'll repack the game while you speak to our jailer." She couldn't ask him out for lunch again, not after the last disaster, so this would be the final time she saw him for the year. He'd get a hearty Christmas handshake on her way out the door. Michelle would get a double hug for her antics. Ginger didn't know what Michelle's motivation was, but locking two people in a room wasn't the right way to go about things. Still, Ginger appreciated the results.

She heard Frank at the intercom. "Okay, Michelle, we played the game. It's time to unlock the door."

"Not yet. You didn't see the clue."

"What clue?"

"The one on the bottom."

Ginger flipped the game box over and found an envelope taped to the bottom. She removed the enclosed paper before Frank had a chance to rejoin her and began reading. "Uh-oh."

CHAPTER 4

"I'M GOING to be grounded forever. Like, until I'm sixteen. Dad's going to put bars on the windows and lock me in my room," Michelle Cardinal said.

Paul Cardinal suspected there weren't enough bars in Kenora to make that happen. He dropped his hand on Michelle's head. "If this doesn't work, I'll be grounded right alongside you." Then he crouched beside her and gave her a hug. "But don't worry. This will work. I know it." Between the two of them, they had to be more stubborn than his son. Although it would be a close call.

He watched his son over the silent security monitor. The waving hands and red face did not bode well, but Ginger's laugh seemed to calm Frank down. He and Michelle were keeping an eye on the pair in the workshop for safety's sake, but they'd agreed to let Frank and Ginger have their privacy.

Paul led Michelle to the light pine kitchen table, where lunch was waiting. The toasted half-bagel smeared with cream cheese, a bunch of grapes, and four carrot sticks must have appealed, because she climbed onto her chair and dove in. "You're sure this will work, right, Grandpa?"

"I'm sure. Your father is exactly like I was at his age, and this kind of situation is just like how I ended up dating your grandmother. All he needs is a little encouragement. That's what we're giving him."

"How did you meet Grandma?"

Paul couldn't help but smile. Michelle was more like the grandmother she'd never met than she realized. It was more than the waves in her dark hair or the twinkle in her brown eyes. "I was impressed with her the moment I saw her. She was a real trailblazer. It was a big deal that she was an Ojibwe reporter on a newspaper staff, so I already knew her name. The night I met her for the first time in person, she was hot on the trail of a story, and I was in the way."

━━

The twenty-four-hour gas station on Highway 17 had horrible coffee, but horrible was better than nothing, so twenty-five-year-old Paul Cardinal pulled up to the diner part of the gas station-restaurant building to refill his thermos and take the opportunity to get out of the cab of his truck. He'd been plowing lanes and parking lots around Kenora since ten o'clock that night. Now it was two in the morning, and he had another three hours to go, as long as the snow didn't start again.

He enjoyed doing seasonal maintenance work most of the year. Watching the world burst into green in the spring and being part of that by filling gardens with seeds and flowers. Spending all day outside in the summer, mowing lawns under the sun. Enjoying the beautiful colours of fall as he raked yards and prepared garden beds for a few months' rest. But the bills didn't stop in the winter, which meant he had to be out in the cold when everyone else was asleep, ensuring roads were passable so people could safely continue with their lives while Mother Nature tried to bury them under northern Ontario snow.

Sometimes it felt like he was alone in the world: him and Agnes and Tim, the diner's night-shift waitress and short-order cook. Agnes returned his Thermos and Paul returned to his truck with the intention of heading to the high school's parking lot. He made it to the corner before he had to hit the brakes.

Frank leaned over the steering wheel to get a better look at the large, shadowy figure. It was too big to be a car and too small to be a semi. It might be a pickup with a cap over the box. It didn't matter; whatever it was, it shouldn't be blocking the road. He tapped the horn but got no reaction.

He debated getting out of his truck to see what the problem was, but he didn't get the chance. A set of head-lights approached from the other direction. A gust of wind raised the newly fallen snow into a cloud that blocked visibility for a blink of time, and when it cleared, the shadow was gone.

The other car kept coming, rolling to a stop when their vehicles aligned. His white pick-up dwarfed the tiny red Pacer. The other driver's window rolled down. "You haven't seen a moose around here, have you?" the woman behind the wheel asked.

"What?"

"A moose. Tall. Furry. Four legs. Antlers."

It was funny; she looked normal. Gorgeous but

normal. Paul's eyes were first drawn to her lips, which were a shocking but unnatural shade of red. When he looked up from her smile, he saw a beautiful pair of brown eyes behind the largest glasses he'd ever seen. She was so pretty he forgot how to speak. "I know what a moose is," he eventually got out.

"So, did you see one?" she asked again.

"A moose? In Kenora?"

The woman held a business card out of the window. *Molly Brown, Reporter/photographer, Kenora Weekly Sentinel.* "I got a tip that a moose has been sighted in town twice since Monday. The reports say it is only out at night. I'm trying to confirm it for a story. Have you seen one or not?"

"No."

"You're the first person I've seen out after midnight. In fact, you're the only person I've seen out, which isn't surprising, considering how much snow we've been getting." She spoke at a mile a minute, her voice reminding him of music. "If you do spot him, call the newspaper. If I'm not there, leave a message on the machine with the details, and I'll get there as soon as I can. What's your name?"

"Paul. Paul Cardinal. Cardinal Outdoor Services."

"Well, Paul Cardinal, I'd love to get a call from you some time." Molly closed the window and continued down the street. She was gone as quickly as she arrived, and another gust of wind immediately buried her tire tracks, leaving him to wonder if she—or the shadow—had ever existed at all.

———

Michelle looked at him expectantly. "That's it? That's the whole story?"

"Yep."

"Why didn't she give you her cell phone number?"

"Cell phones didn't exist in 1984."

His granddaughter stared at him. "How did you live?"

Paul howled in laughter at the horrified look on her face. "I assure you, little miss, that civilization rolled on quite effectively before the invention of the cell phone." For a moment, he felt a little sympathy for Michelle. She'd never know the anticipation of haunting the post office for a letter or planning a trip with a paper map spread across the kitchen table.

"So, she gave you her phone number, and you called her at work and asked her out, and that's the end of the story?"

That would have been much too easy. "No, I never called her."

━━

Paul didn't see the shadow or the reporter again for two days. At midnight on the third evening, he pulled into the Husky diner and spotted a familiar red car in the parking lot.

Molly had taken over a booth. Her spiral notebook sat on the edge of the tabletop, a cup of steaming coffee beside it. The rest of the table was covered in notes and maps and highlighters which threatened to roll onto the floor at any minute. When a yellow one tried to make a getaway, Frank swooped in and caught it before it hit the floor.

"Thanks."

"You're welcome. Are you still on the trail of the mystery moose?" He slid his Thermos across the counter to Agnes, who took it with a smile.

"You mean the ghost reindeer?"

"It's a ghost reindeer, now?"

Molly nodded. "There was another report. It was seen again at night. This one had a decent description of the size and antlers. It's definitely not a moose. It's a caribou or an elk, which are the same family as reindeer. But this time, it left hoofprints outside a bedroom window." She handed him a slip of paper. "What does this say? I can't read my own handwriting."

"Petersen. 38 Rabbit Lake Road."

"Right. The Petersens. They reported that they saw a white form moving away from the house. When they went out to check, they found hoofprints by the window."

"I didn't think ghosts left footprints," Paul said, confused at the logic.

"Apparently it vanished like a ghost, and there were no tracks leading *away* from the house."

"Okay, it was a ghost. But how did an elk turn into a reindeer?"

She laughed. "Apparently they told their son that the reindeer was sent by Santa to spy on him and make sure he was in bed when he was supposed to be. The son insisted that the RCMP report state the peeper was a reindeer working for St. Nick."

Agnes returned with his Thermos, and he slid into the other side of the booth. "That's cute, but why is the paper reporting it as a reindeer?" he asked.

Molly sighed. "Because my editor also thinks it's cute and would be a good page three article so close to Christmas. I need a photo to run with the story. You're one of the few people I've met who is regularly up at night, which is the only time our ghost reindeer has been sighted. Are you sure you haven't seen anything?"

He wanted to lie, because the truth meant he might not have another reason to join her for coffee. But the truth won out. "I'm sure." But he realized that didn't have to be the end of the conversation. "Let me see that address again."

Paul noted the location of the Petersen house on the map and compared it to two other Xs penciled on the paper. "You've seen the pattern to these sightings, haven't you?"

"There's a pattern?"

He took the opportunity to slide around to the other bench so they could sit side by side. "Your ghost reindeer is working its way down Rabbit Lake Road to Veterans Drive. It should hit the intersection in the next night or two."

"That's not good. If it goes south instead of north, it'll head deeper into town and really start to cause problems." A caribou wasn't nearly as big as a moose, which could take on a car and win, but it would still cause a lot of damage to an unsuspecting driver who came upon it in the dead of night.

"At least you know where to look now."

"Yes, thank you. All I need now is a working car heater, so I don't freeze to death waiting for it to show up. It's supposed to storm again tomorrow."

This was his chance to ask her out. It would be a work date, not a date-date. Unless she wanted to call it that. He wouldn't mind. "Then I'll definitely be out and about. Would you..." Paul's courage gave out. "Would you like me to call you if I see it?"

Her brown eyes got big. "Or you could let me drive around town with you. I could be the spotter. I won't interfere with your job at all, I promise." She waited for him to respond, and when he said nothing, she sweetened the deal. "I'll bring snacks."

It wasn't necessary, but he wasn't about to turn them down. "That could work too."

CHAPTER 5

FRANK TOOK the recycled envelope with trepidation, then double-checked to make sure no more little additions were hiding at the bottom. He had no idea what Michelle had in store, but he knew it would be imaginative. "This is what I mean. She needs to be challenged at school, so she'll be less challenging at home. I can barely keep up with her. What kind of kid comes up with a scheme like this?".

Ginger laughed. "I don't know. Every kid who has ever seen *Home Alone?*"

He loved his daughter, which was what made it so frustrating. He wanted the best for her, but providing it where they were was a problem. So far, he hadn't come up with a workable compromise. Still, it did his heart good to see her acting like a kid and not a pint-sized adult. "What does it say?"

Ginger scanned it, then frowned slightly. She handed it to him, and he read it aloud. "Dear Dad, since you have been too busy to put up the workshop tree, I've decided you two have to do it. Today. You need more Christmas spirit, and Ginger is just the helper you need. The tree and lights and ornaments are in the cleaning closet."

"Come on, I'll show you where the closet is." The second they were out of sight of the camera, he shook his hands at the ceiling. The scheming pair of them! His own father was part of this setup. Michelle didn't say anything to implicate her grandfather, but she couldn't have retrieved the boxed Christmas tree from the garage rafters without grown-up help. Aside from his ribbing, his dad had been pretty quiet about Frank's feelings for Ginger. But inviting Ginger to decorate with him would make an intimate moment between them, forever tying her to the Cardinal family holidays. "What's wrong?" she asked.

Frank froze. He couldn't very well say that his family was pushing him to ask Ginger on a date. That was worse than locking them in a room together. If she knew his hand was being forced, she'd be rightly insulted that he was being forced to do it. It was unfair to both of them.

He would have worked up to asking her out eventually. If he didn't get around to it today, he would have put on his list of New Year's resolutions. Right after finding Michelle a new school and before demolishing the old gardening shed and building a new one. It wasn't a matter of desire; it was all about the timing, and this wasn't the right time.

His family, apparently, had other ideas.

Not to mention, they were making him look bad. "I want you to know I'm not channeling Scrooge. The main tree in the house has been up since the last weekend of November. Plus, Michelle has her own little one in her room. And we put up all the lights on the house. I have a ton of Christmas spirit! Michelle was the one who kept putting off helping me decorate the workshop. Now I know why."

Her green eyes widened in surprise. "Frank, of everything I could say about you, lacking Christmas spirit isn't one of them. For heaven's sake, you design games for a living. You have a workshop that is every young-at-heart person's dream. And you put out a new toy for Christmas every year! Not to mention, your house always looks amazing. It's a highlight of my year to come here in December and see what you've done with it."

He hadn't realized she noticed. "My mom loved Christmas. So did Jennifer, Michelle's mom." He appreciated that it didn't hurt to say her name anymore. It had taken a long time to get over his wife's death. Doing it with a newborn daughter had made it both easier and harder.

"It sounds like Michelle gets it from all the women in her family. I'm sorry I never had a chance to meet Jennifer."

Was it weird to talk about your dead wife with a woman you wanted to ask out? A little, but it would be stranger to pretend she didn't exist. Jennifer would always be part of his life, and Michelle's. "She was really quiet. It was one of the reasons we got along so well. We were alike that way. She'd be just as stumped at Michelle's personality as I am, but she would be one hundred percent involved in her schooling."

"May I ask what happened to her?" Ginger asked quietly.

"Jennifer was in good shape, but she developed gestational diabetes when she was pregnant. She did everything right, but she and the doctors were unable to get it under control after Michelle was born. Her body just refused to cooperate with science and medicine. She passed away a little more than a year later."

"That's horrible. I'm so sorry."

"Me too. I wish Michelle had a chance to know her mom. My dad and I do our best. We have movies and pictures. We're still trying to digitize some of them." He laughed. "Michelle gets so offended when we have to pull out the old VCR. I'm ninety-nine percent sure she's going into computer engineering so she can discover a way to download things right into her brain."

"She probably will, and I can't remember to carry my phone with me. All our hopes lie with the next generation, Frank."

"They'd better. They certainly don't lie with the generation who let themselves get locked in a workshop by a nine-year-old."

"Hey!" Ginger protested.

"You're locked in here with me."

"Fair enough."

The boxes were exactly were Michelle said they would be. She'd even swept around them to ensure they were impossible to miss in the small storage room. The artificial tree came in three parts. The lights and ornaments were hand-me-downs from the house's main tree: strings with a few burned out bulbs, and a nearly complete set of Elsa blue and silver balls from when his daughter was going through her Frozen phase. His father must have added the box of candy canes. They never would have let food sit in a storage area for a year.

When he pulled out a tangled ball of wires, Ginger helped him for a while. They got the lights stretched out and unraveled. But rather than help him wind them around the tree, which they'd set near the window, she picked up the candy canes and walked back to the security camera. She tore the cellophane off the box, and carefully removed a candy cane. Then she took that wrapping off and, miming great delight and excitement, took a big bite of the stick. She rubbed her stomach and Frank could practically hear the silent "Yummy!" she performed.

"What are you doing?"

"I'm eating Michelle's decorations. I don't suppose she left a box of gingerbread cookies to be hung on the tree, did she? I'm starving."

He'd forgotten Ginger had been on the road for three hours already. "We should hurry so you can get some lunch."

"I'll be fine. I'm just yanking her chain a little." Then she grinned. "Let's put all the candy canes at the top where she can't reach them."

"You are mean!" But she was also funny. "Let's do it."

The thin pencil tree didn't take long to decorate. Once it was up, the smart-Alec duo in the house piped Christmas music through the intercom speaker. Ginger quickly got into bop-along mode while she hung balls haphazardly on her half of the tree. Then she disappeared again, saying she had an idea. While she was gone, he tried to rearrange some of Ginger's ornament placements to make the tree more symmetrical.

"Please tell me you aren't using a ruler to make them equidistant apart," she begged as she busted him adjusting a ball for the third time.

"Of course not."

Rather than get offended, she let him finish, although she did look at him and smile more often than he thought was necessary. A few minutes later, the tree displayed a well-balanced mix of blue and silver.

When he stepped back to look at the tree from a distance, she showed him the bucket full of fake red roses that had been sitting on a shelf in the corner for as long as Frank could remember. "Can we use these?" she asked.

"Sure."

Ginger slipped them among the branches, trying to keep them evenly spaced. Considering how randomly she'd hung the first set of ornaments, he knew the extra care was for his benefit, and he appreciated it. The little bursts of red added colour he hadn't realized had been missing. "I wouldn't have thought of adding those."

"I have a cousin who is a florist in B.C. She does amazing things with all kinds of flowers in Christmas displays. I thought I'd take a chance." She added another rose, then said out of nowhere, "I'd rock around this Christmas tree."

He stared at her. It was a completely un-Ginger-like thing to say. When she saw his puzzled look, she tapped her ear, and he listened hard for a moment. "Rockin' Around the Christmas Tree" was playing in the background.

"Okay, Ginger, show me what you've got."

Despite her words, she was not actually prepared to rock. She shuffled her feet a little and did a sad little spin.

"That won't do at all." Frank twisted over to her, his hips swiveling to the beat. He took her arm, spun her out, pulled her back, and caught her free hand in his. He proceeded to dance her around the Christmas tree, swinging and swaying as Brenda Lee sang about a myriad of holiday traditions. He gratefully realized that Michelle and his father had missed an opportunity; there hadn't been any mistletoe in the box. That would have pushed the awkwardness of the situation over the top.

The song ended and a weather report came on. Frank didn't hear a word of it. A tornado could be coming for all he cared because he had one arm around her waist and was still holding her hand.

"I didn't know you could do that," she said breathlessly.

"It's all in the partner."

"It certainly is," she agreed.

They finished the tree beautifully. But that was when he realized he'd made a terrible mistake. He'd rushed through decorating the tree so Ginger could get some lunch, but now she was free to go and have lunch. Without him, since she'd never asked him again, and he hadn't asked her either.

Frank took a breath, about to rectify that colossal double error, when the speaker clicked on again.

"Hi, Daddy. I can only see part of the tree on the camera, but I looked at it through the window, too, and I like it. Ginger, the roses are really pretty," Michelle's voice said.

Ginger shot a thumbs-up at the camera.

"I liked the dancing too. It was *so* romantic."

Frank did not need his sweet little daughter getting any ideas. She shouldn't be thinking about romance at her age anyway. "How about letting us out now? We finished the tree. Poor Ginger hasn't eaten since breakfast, except for that candy cane, and it's well past lunch time," Frank said. The first two delays had been cute, barely. But now getting out of there was a necessity.

"Don't worry, Dad. I thought of that."

"Oh, no," Ginger said quietly.

He agreed.

INTERLUDE

North Pole Unlimited Headquarters,
    December, Manitoba, Canada (25 kilometres south-east of Winnipeg)

She wasn't acting guilty. She hadn't done anything wrong. But Jilly Lewis shut the door to her office and made sure her boss was gone before she picked up the phone and dialed.

"Good morning, Cardinal residence," the male voice at the other end of the call said.

"Hi, Paul. It's Jilly. How's it going?"

See? Totally innocent question. A question any friend would ask another with nothing nefarious inferred.

"Today is shaping up to be a great day. Ginger arrived safely this morning and she and Frank are in the workshop right now."

"That's good to hear." So far, it sounded like everything was going according to plan. "Are they having a business meeting?" Even though the conversation was innocuous so far, Jilly kept an eye on the door. She'd promised her fiancé that she'd take a step back from matchmaking at Christmas this year and concentrate on her own upcoming wedding, but old habits were hard to break. Besides, technically, she was keeping her word.

She wasn't doing the matchmaking. She was simply providing moral support.

Paul cleared his throat. She thought she heard a snicker before he did it again. "No. I could hardly believe it when my angelic granddaughter locked them in the workshop together after stealing their phones," he said.

"Oh, my, that's terrible!" *Terribly effective.* She definitely didn't plan to use that idea herself in the future.

"She's created a list of activities they have to do together before she's letting them out. I think she called it a quest."

She loved this kid. "Like what?"

When Paul had originally contacted her, Jilly thought it was with a contract question. In fact, when he identified himself, she immediately reached for the contact list for the legal department. Indie-Genius Games was a valued partner; if there was a problem Jilly was going to take care of it without messing around. But it had turned out to be a personal call.

Paul had heard—somehow—that she'd had a bit of luck getting compatible people together in a romantic way, and he wanted advice. Jilly tried to claim that she didn't do that anymore, but when he explained the desperate situation after his son's accidental gaff in the spring, she couldn't refuse. It was the season of giving, and advice for the lovelorn was something she had in abundance.

Jilly thought the only thing Frank needed was another opportunity to be alone with Ginger. She'd known the other woman for a couple years; Ginger wasn't the type to hold a grudge. She was the cautious sort, though. After being turned down so sharply, she was going to retreat. It would be up to Frank to take the lead the next time. After that conversation, Paul called her back a couple weeks later and they had a conversation about when he and Michelle—and Frank—could expect to see Ginger in Kenora again. Jilly found a way to send her the next week.

"You know how Ginger was coming up to pick up the prototype of Catch Me If You Can? Michelle thought they should test it first, so she made them play the game. Judging from the jumping and arm waving, Ginger won."

"You spied through the window?"

"No, we watched over the security camera."

"I am a rank amateur," Jilly muttered to herself. She also said it aloud because Paul chuckled.

"We aren't listening in. I insisted they have some privacy."

Jilly coughed.

"I mean, Michelle gave them some privacy while leaving the camera on for safety reasons."

"Of course, for safety."

"Then she told them they had to decorate a Christmas tree together, working as a team. They just finished. We're very encouraged as they head into stage three, because they ended up dancing around the Christmas tree to the holiday music we piped into the workshop," Paul bragged.

Jilly harrumphed. She'd never gotten any of her victi —prospective couples to dance with each other during phase one of her plans. She truly did have to start taking notes from a nine-year-old.

A thump on her office door made her heart skip. "One second," she whispered into the phone. She set the receiver on her desk and opened the door.

Joy Harness was leaning against the wall. The purse on her arm swung and bounced off the doorframe, repeating the sound. "Sorry, Jilly. I stepped to the side to get a breather for a minute." She placed a hand on her pregnant belly. "This little bean isn't due for another month, but I think I'm going to need a wheelbarrow to get around by then," she joked.

"Do you want to come in and sit down for a bit?" The Veterinary Services wing was on the other side of the North Pole Unlimited compound, which was a long trek on swollen ankles.

"No thanks. I have to get my steps in. Besides, I'm going to stop at the security office and have lunch with Decker while he's on his break. Apparently, a hacker is trying to get into our systems, looking for Santa's naughty and nice list." Her brown eyes sparked. "Good luck to them getting past my husband."

"You'd think they'd learn," Jilly agreed. There seemed to be an annual attempt to hack the customer list at Santa's #1 store on the internet. It was usually tracked back to a talented elementary school student with too much time and not enough supervision.

"Besides, it looks like I caught you in the middle of a call." Joy lifted her chin and indicated the phone on Jilly's desk. "Did I interrupt anything important?"

Jilly shook her head. "Locksmithing discussion."

"Oh, don't worry about it. Andrea found the spare key to the storage room in her desk. Then she found the original key on a shelf inside the storage room. Now everything is back in its proper place."

"I won't have anyone come out then."

Joy pushed herself off the wall and found her equilibrium. "I'm off like a herd of turtles. See you tomorrow at the wrap party at the church?"

"I'll be there with bells on," Jilly promised.

She waited until Joy rounded the corner, slammed her door shut, and raced back to the desk. "Sorry about that. It was a false alarm. What's stage three?" Jilly asked.

"A romantic lunch for two."

"That sounds nice."

"Michelle planned it."

"Why do I hear hesitation in your voice?"

"She won't tell me what she packed. She insisted on doing it by herself. All I was allowed to do was provide the dessert, since it was something that she couldn't do without Frank cottoning on." Paul sighed. "I have a sneaking suspicion it's PB and J finger sandwiches. Grape."

Jilly howled. It was too perfect. That was definitely a child's version of fancy. Plus, it would completely eliminate her as a suspect. "I love it."

"We'll see if Frank and Ginger are as understanding."

"Good luck to all of you. Let me know how it goes."

"We will, Jilly. Thanks."

She'd just hung up the phone when her door opened without a warning knock. Luckily for him, the man who stuck his head in was an excellent kisser. "Have you had lunch yet?"

"No." She pulled her purse from the lower desk drawer and swung it over her shoulder. She kissed Ben Fredericks when she got to the door, brushing a lock of his more-salt-than-pepper hair off his cheek.

"I thought we weren't going to do that at work."

She pointed up, to where she'd pinned a sprig of mistletoe above the door. "You're just hanging out here. What am I supposed to do? Ignore tradition?"

"What if I was Nick? Or Decker? Or Hollis visiting?"

"I'd tell them to move." She slipped her arm into his. "Let's hit the cafeteria. Do you think they could make me a peanut butter and jelly sandwich?"

CHAPTER 6

PAUL WATCHED Michelle tap the end of her carrot stick on her plate. She'd been impatiently waiting for him to finish his phone call. She had no idea that he'd sought backup on Plan Dad Needs a Date. She was still focused on the story about him and Molly. "Did Grandma bring snacks on your date?" she asked.

"Yes and no. Your grandma brought the most delicious ginger-molasses cookies I'd ever had in my life, but it wasn't a date. We were both working."

"Did you find the ghost reindeer that night?"

"Not even close. But we still found a story for her newspaper."

———

The weather had been unseasonably mild for a week, hovering at the freezing mark during the day. But as soon as the sun went down and the temperature dropped, a fresh layer of snow fell over the area. And it wasn't a light, fluffy snow. It was the heavy, wet stuff that turned into slush the second anything touched it. Paul had his work cut out for him.

Molly didn't seem to mind. After a thorough inspection of his truck, which included his FM radio (which only pulled in three stations), she tossed her cream-coloured toque onto the dashboard. "How long will it take you to do your route?" she asked.

"About three hours," Paul said. It sounded like a long time to be trapped with a person he didn't know well. What if she wanted to talk about the Rough Riders the entire time? She wasn't cute enough for that.

It turned out she didn't even like football.

What Molly liked was cameras. As he nodded along and made encouraging sounds, she told him all about the new F-1 Canon 35mm she was saving for, including the special lenses and flashes she wanted.

"So, you're more of a photographer-slash-reporter than a reporter-slash-photographer?" he asked after a lengthy explanation of the importance of battery life.

"I'd prefer to be a photographer-slash-photographer, but the paper wants stories to go with the pictures. I've made some other sales though. Reader's Digest bought one of my photos last year, and two this year."

"You've cracked the big leagues."

"Mid leagues," Molly corrected. "I'm still aiming for National Geographic. After that, the Pulitzer Prize for Feature Photography." She sighed. "But until then, it's the Kenora Weekly Sentinel. And only if I can find anything interesting to shoot. Otherwise, this week's front page is going to feature the Ontario Junior Figure Skating medal presentation."

Paul took a break at midnight, pulling into the diner. Molly ordered each of them a hot chocolate and a piece of pie "to keep their energy up," and when they were done, they headed back out to finish his plowing for the night.

"Absolutely nothing," she said after he parked the truck after clearing the high school parking lot. "What a disappointment."

"We could go looking," he suggested. The three hours he'd been dreading had passed in the blink of an eye. Now he had to scramble to find an excuse not to end the night so early. "We can check the highway and see if your elk managed to find his way out of town." Although most of the two-lane highway had been literally blown out of the rocky Canadian Shield, there were still sections of open areas where the wild land and ponds came right up to the shoulder.

"Sure, let's take a look."

The snow had stopped, and the clouds had moved on. Now, the clear moonlit night let them see almost as well as on a cloudy day. A couple of trucks passed them, heading toward the Manitoba border. Molly switched off the radio. The hum of the tires on concrete was the only sound around them. The peacefulness of the night was soothing. Until she leaned forward and rapidly cranked down the window. "Did you hear that?" she demanded.

"No, what?" He rolled down his own window. Then he heard it. "Is that hoof beats on asphalt? Do elks have hooves that would sound like that?" A distinct clatter of something hard hitting the road echoed off the granite rock-faces lining the highway. But it wasn't the sound of an animal loping at a steady pace. It was more irregular.

"Brakes!" Molly yelled as they rounded a curve.

His foot was moving before he had time to think. A lifetime of being on the lookout of deer on the side of the road who could bolt into traffic at any time had trained him for this moment, but he didn't see any yellow eyes in the glare of his headlights. What he did see was a large boulder sitting on the double yellow line. Paul slammed the gearshift into reverse and threw his arm over the back of the seat. He hit the gas, and they flew backward for a few yards until they were clear of the cut-through. Thankfully, he didn't see headlights coming from either direction. "That was too close."

"It almost hit us. What do you think happened?"

Paul set his flashers and pulled as far onto the shoulder as he could. "I think with these milder temperatures, snow melted and worked its way into cracks in the rocks. Then, when it froze, it expanded and made the cracks bigger. Rinse and repeat for a couple days, and the cracks became big enough for pieces to break off."

"That sounds reasonable." Molly shivered, and he knew it had nothing to do with the cold.

"We have to warn people. I have flares in my toolkit in the back."

The boulder was in the middle of the road, which meant smaller vehicles could probably swerve around it. But there weren't that many smaller vehicles out at this hour. It was almost exclusively semi-trucks. An accident would block traffic in both directions for hours. "I'll run to set a warning on the far side of the road first." It was the more dangerous option, but he didn't want to risk Molly getting hit by more falling rocks.

"Okay, I'll do this side."

Paul sprinted down the highway, hoping it stayed

clear for a while longer. He dropped the first road flare on the far side of the slide, ten feet before the rock face started. He set another, a hundred feet after that, and a third a further hundred feet past that, where it could be seen by anyone approaching the curve. He hoped it was enough. As soon as they were back in town, he'd contact the local police and let them know about the rockslide, so they could put out warnings.

As he approached his truck, he could see flares spread out in the other direction. But Molly was standing in the middle of the road, camera in hand. She lowered it when he got to her. "Being onsite for a rockslide is much better than a podium picture for the front page. Between the moonlight and the flares, I think there was enough light to make it a really good shot."

He'd been running down the centre of the highway. "I hope I didn't get in your way."

"You were in exactly the right place."

▭

Paul picked up Michelle's plate and carried it to the sink, where he gave it a quick rinse before putting it in the dishwasher.

"Did the newspaper use one of Grandma's pictures?" Michelle asked.

"Oh, yes. On the front page." She'd caught him walking down around the boulder, with a lit flare in his hand, held out to one side. The black-and-white photo the Sentinel put on the front page made him look like a silhouette of a road worker marking the site. The original photo, in colour, had been much cooler. The blue moonlight, combined with the orange glare of the flare, illuminated details that were lost in the newspaper's grainy copy and gave the entire shot an ethereal quality. Molly had hung it in her office for years until the colours faded.

"Did you get a picture of the ghost reindeer?"

"No. Not that night."

CHAPTER 7

IF SHE SET ASIDE the whole *locked in a room and couldn't leave if she wanted to* aspect, Ginger had been having a good time with Frank. He was obviously still uncomfortable, but that seemed to be more with the situation rather than being with her, which was an improvement over their last couple of tense meetings. He was sharing personal stuff. Even if he wasn't interested in anything more, it was nice to get to know him better as a friend.

Michelle's latest revelation crossed the line from funny into ridiculous. Ginger was pretty sure that Paul wouldn't let his granddaughter go on much longer, knowing Ginger had a long drive back to December.

She leaned past Frank and pressed the speaker button. "What do you mean you 'thought of that,' Michelle?"

"You've been working hard this morning, so I made you lunch. I put the food in the fridge. There are extra plates and stuff in the box on the counter. It's a Christmas feast. Once you're finished, I'll let you out."

"No more tricks, Michelle. Or there will be consequences."

"This is the last thing. I promise."

Ginger beat Frank to the punch. "Don't even think of apologizing again. Just feed me. I'm starving."

"You take our lunch out of the fridge. I'll clear some space on my worktable for plates and glasses."

"I'll help you get that ready first."

He tidied—stacking papers, scooping pieces and dice into jars—while she hefted the helpfully labeled "Christmas Party Dishes" box from the counter to the freshly wiped wooden tabletop.

She pulled the flap of the cardboard box and blinked.

"What's wrong?"

"I'm starting to agree that Michelle had help with this little plot of hers." Because the first thing she pulled out was a white tablecloth embroidered with holly and berries around the edges. Beside it were two matching cloth napkins wrapped around two crystal champagne flutes. "Either your father gave her a hand, or she's going to be grounded until next Christmas for messing with your good china."

Frank groaned. "I was hoping I was wrong, but my dad is definitely a co-conspirator."

"I'm flattered." Even if Frank wasn't interested, her heart was warmed with the knowledge that his family would approve.

Ginger helped spread the tablecloth and then handed over the flutes. Next came plain plates; a pretty, glossy white with no design on them. The two cheese knives had her raising an eyebrow, but she gamely set them out beside the small forks they'd been given. The last thing she drew from the box was a vase with a tasteful bouquet of silk flowers. "I don't know, it looks like a restaurant to me."

"It's not bad for a workshop. Are you ready to eat?"

"I'm starving."

Paul may have helped with the dishes, but the food was all Michelle. Ginger had to close the fridge door and hold onto the countertop so she didn't collapse with laughter. "What? Did they have something catered? It's not from Troutman's Pier, is it?" Frank asked.

"No. This was prepared by Chef Michelle Cardinal. Would you like to see what she has prepared for our feast?" Because she'd lost it at the first course. She couldn't wait to see what else was coming.

Ginger slipped the individually labeled entrees onto each palm and carried them to the table like she was a waiter at a Michelin-starred restaurant. "Our main course, monsieur." The Lunchables were festively tied with ribbons and had a green and red bow on them, respectively.

Frank opened his mouth, as if to sigh, but closed it and simply shook his head. "Of course, she did. What else do we have?"

One plastic container was filled with grapes to share, and another with cherry tomatoes and celery sticks: because, as the next Post-it read, they were red and green and more Christmas-y together. Two mini cheese balls wrapped in red wax, and a baggie of crackers to spread it on, which explained the cheese knives. "Oh, fancy. She gave us cranberry ginger ales."

"I love those! It's a shame they're only available at Christmas."

"Me too. And now, dessert."

"I'm terrified," Frank groaned while Ginger reached to the back of the low fridge.

"Why?"

"Michelle has been eating a piece of holiday Rice Krispie cake every day for the last two months. Ever since they came out for the season. I think the grocery store had to double their marshmallow orders just to cover her obsession. I can't even stomach the smell anymore. My dad has to be in the kitchen with her when she makes them."

"I don't think that will be a problem." She returned with a proper bakery box, sealed with a gold foil sticker. "It looks like somebody went all out on dessert. Paul strikes again?"

"He would have had to drive her to the bakery at the very least, or bought them himself, so yes, he's in deep trouble."

"I'm not going to open it yet. Let's let it tempt us." She was a sucker for a surprise. And for dessert. Besides, in a worst-case scenario, she didn't mind Rice Krispie cake. Or she hadn't the last time she'd had a piece, which was about a decade ago.

She let Frank pull out her chair and seat her at their makeshift table. She pulled the napkin from the top of the wineglass and fluffed it before dropping it in her lap. As she peeled the cover from her cheese and cracker tray, something he'd said earlier hit her. "What did you mean, you hoped it wasn't catered from Troutman's Pier?" Had she scared him off so badly that he couldn't even eat there anymore?

"It's been shut down twice in the last year by the sanitation department. I don't know how they manage to keep reopening," he said with a shutter.

Ginger decided that was a good time to open the cheese ball. She was horrified to hear that the restaurant she'd invited him to for lunch had been closed for health code violations. No wonder he'd turned her down flat.

Conversation stalled until Frank asked if she wanted to trade a couple of her ham slices for two of his pepperonis, which lead to a heated debate about pineapple on pizza, which they agreed wasn't a proper topping at all, which led to his family's upcoming trip to Hawaii over the Christmas holiday.

"Once the prototype of Catch Me If You Can has been delivered, I guess you're good for a whole year until you need to get to work again," Ginger said.

"That would be true, except..." He hesitated and blushed deep enough for her to notice on his mahogany skin, I've been thinking about expanding Indie-Genius Games."

"Expanding? Really? Into what?"

"No matter what I pick for Michelle's school, there are going to be extra expenses. I have access to a bunch of my mother's photographs. She did a lot of nature shots. Since jigsaw puzzles are currently going through a resurgence in popularity, I thought producing a line of simple to expert puzzles would be smart."

"That would be a terrific way to go. Honestly, we haven't been able to keep them in stock. If you were going to do it, I'd say start planning and production now, and just jump in. I can send you the numbers when I get back to the office if you're interested." She had all the data on all the toys that North Pole Unlimited offered in their online catalogue, going back as far as the website did. If Frank wanted information further back than that, she'd have to dig through the printed annual reports, but Victor and Adelaide Klassen, the company's founders, hadn't thrown out a scrap of information for the more than four decades they'd been in business. Ginger wouldn't mind. She thrived on data. It made her little number-loving heart sing.

"My online business support group said the same thing. It looks like Indie-Genius Games will be expanding."

Ginger raised her ginger ale-filled champagne flute. "To a wonderful year to come, filled with new opportunities and profit."

"I'm sure that with the help of friends like you, we'll be able to puzzle through any difficulties we run into and come out successful on the other side."

She waited until they had drunk after their toast before she said, "I can't believe you just said, 'puzzle your way through,' and you give me grief for telling bad jokes. Shame on you."

"Now my ego is shattered into five hundred pieces," was his quick reply.

She'd unleashed a monster. "Quit it."

"I don't know if I can put myself back together after that attack."

"Please stop." She didn't know if she could hold back her snicker if he continued, and she didn't want to encourage him.

"I will, but in the future I hope you will look at the complete picture before you criticize my sense of humour."

"How am I supposed to deal with you?"

Frank looked like he was about to speak, but a funny look crossed his face. He opened his mouth again, then snapped it shut. "Shoot! I've run out of puns."

"Don't look at me. I have to consult a joke book before I come to Kenora just so I'm prepared for Michelle."

Then he joined in her laughter. "Seriously, thanks. I've been waffling about moving forward. It's good to know my business sense was on the money. I'll start looking into printers and manufacturers in January."

She wanted to know more, know *everything*. What kinds of pictures did he want to use? What age group did he intended to market to? How many did he want to release? A small part was her business side clapping in glee over the possibilities. The rest was pure excitement about Frank sharing his plans with her. Even better, the way he was talking meant that he intended for North Pole Unlimited, and by extension her, to be part of them, which meant they would continue to work together.

"We still haven't looked at what's in the box," Frank said.

"I can't believe I got so excited about jigsaw puzzles that I forgot about dessert!" She never forgot about dessert, and her worn-out treadmill could testify to that. Ginger didn't need any more encouragement. The cheese knife wasn't sharp enough to cut through the foil sticker with one swipe, but with a little sawing, it finally gave way. She lifted the lid, gave what she hoped was a disappointed smile, and closed the box again. "There must have been some mistake at the bakery. It's empty. I'll take it home with me and recycle the box at my house, so you're not stuck with it."

"Gimme."

"Don't you trust me?"

"Not after watching you devour that candy cane. I think you have a sweet tooth to rival Willie Wonka. What's in the box?"

"You know me too well." She lifted the lid again and tilted the box, revealing luscious icing-sugar topped lemon squares, butter tarts with raisins, and two iced ginger-bread cookies.

"That's a pretty good spread. Does anything particularly appeal?" Frank asked. She noticed his eyes hadn't moved off the butter tarts since he spied them.

"Only the squares, the tarts, and the cookies," she said with a grin.

Frank rifled through the supplies box and came up with two small dessert plates. They dished out their desserts and refilled their flutes. "This is a pleasant surprise after the Lunchables. I'll have to thank my dad."

"My grandmother used to make butter tarts for Christmas. Not my grandma exactly. She was my grand-father's lady friend, but they never got married. She was still part of the family for years until she passed. She always used to worry about not being able to contribute to the holiday meals, but we convinced her that her butter tarts were more than enough." Ginger smiled at the memory. "When she got older, she used to bring grocery store tarts, and we loved them just the same. We could have bought them whenever we wanted to, but we only ate them when she came to visit." Now, whenever she went home, she and her sister argued over who was going to bring Mrs. Acorn's butter tarts. Her brother didn't care, as long as there were some on the dainty tray after a turkey supper. Some Christmas memories were forever.

"I had an aunt who had the same reputation with lemon squares. My dad's sister. I think everyone in the family has a copy of Louise's Lemon Squares. I've already made one for Michelle when she's old enough to start baking on her own. Food can be love, can't it?"

"Absolutely. Family recipes and traditions are priceless." Despite cutting the lemon slice with her knife and fork, the desserts went down much too quickly. They gathered the plates and glasses and cutlery without speaking and washed them all in the workshop sink. Then they carefully rewrapped them and redeposited them back into the box. "Is that it?" Ginger asked. "Are we free to go now?"

"We had better be," Frank said. "Not that I've minded spending the morning with you. At all." Something in his voice made her look up, and she saw regret in his eyes. "But fun and games have a limit, and I know we're already soft on enforcing limits with Michelle. We'll get you on your way. You probably need to get home and prepare for Christmas. It's only a couple weeks away. It sounds like you have a lot of shopping to do for your family."

"My nieces and nephews think I have a direct line to Santa's workshop. I have no idea why," she said with a smile and they both laughed. "I start getting emails in September, so my shopping has been done for a while. But I should get going."

"Then I guess our time together is over."

She felt as disappointed as Frank sounded.

CHAPTER 8

MICHELLE'S BROWN EYES WIDENED. "You found it? It was real? Was it a reindeer or a just a regular deer? When did you find it?"

For a little girl who was so advanced academically, Paul was thrilled to see her acting her age. But, because he was her grandfather, he looked her in the eye and walked to the counter to top off his coffee cup before he resumed his story.

"Grandpa, hurry up," she whined. "What happened?"

"It was the week before Christmas, and your grandmother and I had almost given up hope of tracking down Kenora's ghost reindeer. We'd been looking for over a week," he began.

▭

They hadn't gone out every evening. Paul was used to the night shift, but Molly still had to be in the office every morning, working on other stories for the paper. He'd kept an eye out on the nights she couldn't drive around with him. He swore he'd seen something the night before, so he'd left a message for Molly to call him back when she got to the office the next morning. Sure enough, at nine in the morning, which was the middle of the night for him, his house phone rang incessantly until he stumbled to the kitchen to pick it up. "Hello?"

"Where did you see it?"

No greeting, no name, just a demand for a reindeer update. "Good morning to you too, Molly."

She just laughed. "Where was it, Paul?"

"Exactly where we thought it would be. I think it was headed downtown."

"Oh no, that's totally the wrong direction. We have to get it turned around."

"We need to find it first. Preferably tonight. Tomorrow is the deadline for submitting stories and photos, isn't it?" Paul had learned there was fierce competition for the front-page story of the week. Molly was one of three reporters vying for it, plus the newspaper's editor, who also submitted the occasional story. This was the second-last paper of the year, and the last one before Christmas. If she was going to get a shot, tonight was the night it would count the most. "Grab a nap after work, and I'll pick you up at eight o'clock sharp. We'll drive until we find Kenora's ghost reindeer or we run out of night."

The warm winter weather had finally given way to regular temperatures, leaving a clear night sky. The moon was down to three-quarters full, but between it and the streetlights, they had no trouble looking far up the town's lanes and crescents, hoping for a glimpse of their elusive prey.

Their bad luck held until midnight. Then they turned onto Main Street. A light wind picked up, lifting fluffy snowflakes off the roofs of the businesses, and letting them drift back to the street. They saw the occasional figure: one person walking their dog, two others heading to the lakeside for what Paul assumed was a romantic stroll.

And there was one large figure outside Kripke's window. Kripke's was an odd store; it primarily focused on campers and tourists during the summer, but it was open all year round. If a vacationer needed something for their tent or cottage and couldn't eat it, they could find it at Kripke's. Frying pans, replacement tent poles, and inner tube patch kits. The store also had a whole section of sporting gear, games, and activities. Over the winter, that part saw the most activity.

The store's front window was an explosion of hockey sticks, ski poles, and snow saucers. Stuffed animals hung from a pair of crisscrossed skis, and mittens decorated the small Christmas tree in the corner. And standing dead centre out front, blocking the entire sidewalk, was the biggest—reindeer?—Paul had ever seen. The massive buck had an impressive set of antlers, sweeping back from its head rather than curling sideways. Its light brown coat had a slight shine under the streetlights, with shaggy white-beige hair starting behind its ears and stretching down to its front legs.

"Stop the car!"

He was sure Molly meant to whisper, but he was surprised the animal wasn't scared off by the yelling. "I'm stopping. Hold on."

Her fingers fumbled at the seatbelt buckle. "I've got to shoot it before it gets away."

The animal stepped closer to the window. "I think you have time. He seems to be checking out the hockey stick collection." The reindeer–elk?–seemed enamoured by the blinking lights of the display and showed no sign of being spooked. In fact, it took a step sideways, almost posing for Molly as she approached a few steps with her camera in front of her.

"Don't get too close. It's still a wild—"

"Animal," she finished with him. "I know. I just need a couple more." She raised the camera to her cheek, adjusted the focus on the lens, and pressed the shutter button. "I think these are all going to be perfect. The front page of the Christmas edition is mine!" she gloated as she climbed back into the cab of the truck. She leaned over the gear shift and gave him a quick kiss on the cheek. Frank froze, but Molly didn't seem to notice. She was riding the high of getting the shot after a week of fruitless nights.

She held her fingers over the vent pumping hot air onto the windshield.

"I'm glad you got your shots, but we still have a reindeer camped out in downtown Kenora. We can't leave him here." A deer that size could take out a small car. Paul gave the large animal another look and upgraded his concern to mid-sized car. The damage to the reindeer would be minimal.

"What can we do? We can't herd it anywhere, and I don't think it's going to follow us because we ask nicely."

The idea was so funny that Paul had to run with it. He rolled down his window and called across the street in the dead of night, "Excuse me, Mr. Reindeer. We need to get you out of town. Would you like to follow me?"

His eyes almost bugged out of his head when the deer

snorted and tossed its head a couple times. It stepped into the street and pawed at the concrete but held its ground.

"Um, I think he's waiting for you to lead the way," Molly said quietly.

"What do I do?"

"Put the truck in drive and head north, slowly?" she suggested, although her tone meant she was just as flummoxed as him when it came to the next step.

Paul put on his flashers to warn any vehicles they should come across to give him a wide berth. Then he slipped the truck into gear and began rolling up the street. Sure enough, the reindeer fell into a trot behind the truck.

Paul kept his eyes on the road, while Molly craned her neck to keep an eye out the back window. "It's working. It's following us."

"Weirdest. Parade. Ever," Paul muttered. They crawled up the road well under the speed limit, giving the reindeer lots of time, but it didn't look around or wander away. It stayed on his bumper for several long minutes until they turned onto Veterans Drive. But when they drove past the fire station, it veered into the parking lot.

"Stop, you lost him," Molly said, but Paul had already hit the brakes.

"Where did he go?" They'd intended to lead the animal farther north, but if it bolted past the building, it still had a decent chance to find its way back into the wild.

"He..." Molly paused, twisted in her seat. "He stopped at the station's billboard."

"What billboard?"

"The billboard reminding people to get their chimneys checked before they start having winter fires. The one that's been up since September."

Now he knew what she was talking about. It was plain and ugly and one of several that went up in the area reminding folks of basic fire safety tips. They switched to outdoor campfire safety during the summer. "What's he doing now?"

"Reading it, apparently." She paused for a moment. "Hold on, he's moving again." Then a gasp. "He's coming this way."

Before Paul ask what direction, he heard a thump on his window. When he turned his head, he found himself face to snout with the biggest deer he'd ever seen in his life. He'd never been so close to a live one, especially one leaving a nose print on his window, and whose breath was frosting the glass and leaving a cloud in the air around his head.

"Don't move," he whispered.

"I'm not!"

The reindeer trotted back to the sign for a moment, then returned to the truck. This time, it butted its head on the window hard enough to make the glass rattle and the entire vehicle shake.

"What does it want?"

The reindeer returned to the billboard and stood beside it. From the angle of its huge head, it looked like it was reading it. The head moved slightly, to look at them, and then returned to the "reading" position.

"Maybe it's waiting for a picture."

"The reindeer wants me to take a picture of it?" Molly asked in disbelief.

"I'm not going to argue with it. Are you? Take the picture."

Molly huffed but opened her door. She carefully focused on the deer and the sign, then jumped back inside. "Holy cow, it's freezing out there now. The temperature is dropping like a rock."

"But you got the shot?"

"I got the shot," she confirmed. "I don't know why it wanted a picture of itself in front of a *check your chimney* sign, but I got it. Now what?"

Paul had kept his eye on the animal but his ear on the conversation. As soon as Molly was back in the truck, the reindeer resumed its place behind the truck. "I think he's ready for us to finish the trip out of town."

It didn't take long to hit the edge of Kenora. They soon left the town behind. They slowly cruised all the way to the junction at Highway 17 and pulled over to the shoulder before they had to cross it. The reindeer trotted up beside the driver's door again.

Paul rolled down his window a crack. After everything, it only seemed polite. "Okay, buddy, this is it. Keep heading north and you should be fine. And have a merry Christmas."

The reindeer snorted and tossed its head. It pawed the ground a couple times and then galloped away, disappearing when a huge gust, on the otherwise nearly windless evening, blew up a cloud of snow which briefly covered the highway.

They sat in the idling truck, neither speaking for a minute.

"Was that as weird as I think it was?" Molly eventually asked.

"I'm pretty sure it was." Deer or anything like them—moose, elk, reindeer—did not behave like that. They didn't follow humans or approach vehicles. They certainly didn't tap on windows to get people's attention. Weird didn't begin to cover it.

"Well, I got my photos. I owe you a big thank you for that," Molly said.

Paul gulped. That sounded like a goodbye, and he didn't want their time together to end. They'd driven around and talked and had midnight coffee and pie at the diner. If that was over...

It was time to take the plunge. If Molly said no, he'd never see her again, which would suck, but he'd get over it, eventually. But if she said yes, he'd get to see her every day. Was there really a decision?

He could do this. He'd just stared down a reindeer, nose to nose. Asking Molly out face to face couldn't be that much harder.

"Will you be writing a story to go with those pictures?" he asked. He knew she had to spend at least an hour in the darkroom to develop all of tonight's photos. Writing a story would add another half day. In theory, she could be free for supper the next night. Paul gave his head a shake. That didn't take into account the rest of her life, like sleeping and laundry and finishing her last-minute Christmas shopping. She was probably extra busy at this time of year.

Maybe he'd get lucky, and she'd be free for New Year's Eve. But that was two weeks away, and any woman as gorgeous as she was had probably been asked out months ago for one of the biggest party nights of the year.

"You bet. I don't know what I'm going to say, but I'll come up with something." She shrugged, but her smile said she wasn't overly concerned with coming up with an idea.

"Then you'll probably be busy with all you pre-Christmas preparations."

"Nah, I'm all set. I finished my shopping in October.

Once I get this story in, the *Weekly Sentinel* offices close until after the holiday. I'll be on call one day, but aside from that, I'll be as free as a bird until Boxing Day!"

"Then a New Year's Eve party to finish the year?"

"No. I haven't been invited to any yet."

There went all his excuses to put off asking her out. But the timing wasn't right yet.

⌗

Michelle squealed in glee. Since Paul had stopped his story after the reindeer took off into the night, he didn't know what had set her off. "What are you so excited about?"

"I know why the reindeer stopped at the sign and made grandma take a picture of him there! It's because Santa comes down chimneys, and he wanted to remind everybody to make sure it was safe before Christmas Eve. Didn't any of you grown-ups figure that out, Grandpa?" she asked in exasperation.

"Well, I didn't, and your grandma didn't, but her boss did," Paul admitted. "The front page of the *Kenora Weekly Sentinel* that week had two photos. One of the deer in front of the toy display, where he was making sure it was fully stocked in case Santa needed to make an emergency pickup, and the other was of the reindeer reminding people to check their chimneys before Santa's visit." Molly hadn't been thrilled to add those two "facts" to her article about the oversized visitor to town, but the amount of mail the newspaper received afterward convinced her that, at that particular time of year, a little creative license had been more important than pure, unemotional news reporting.

"Did he come back? The reindeer? I don't think he did because his job was done."

"No, he didn't. We never saw him again, not even at another Christmas."

"I'll bet he got in a lot of trouble when he got back to the North Pole." Michelle dug into her pudding cup with gusto. "Do you think maybe he came back, and nobody saw him? Maybe that year was his first time, and he wasn't very good at sneaking."

"Could be. If he did, he was definitely better at not getting caught." Paul still doubted it was a real reindeer. Their size and the sweep of their antlers were distinct from the native wildlife. It wasn't unusual to see a buck with a deformed antler, and it would have made much more sense than having a reindeer, or even an elk running around town. But despite the photographs, the argument remained whenever the stories came out around the old-timers in town.

"What about you and Grandma? Did you ask her out?" she asked as she licked the back of her spoon.

"Not then."

She set her spoon on the table and sighed in exasperation. "Grandpa." She made it sound like it was three sylla-bles. "Why not? Santa sent a reindeer to get you together. Grandma even kissed you. What were you waiting for?"

"I wanted to. She was smarter and prettier and funnier every time I saw her. But it wasn't the right time yet."

CHAPTER 9

FRANK WAS GOING to speak to his daughter and have stronger words with his father. The last couple hours had been torture. Every peek he'd had into Ginger's past only convinced him more that they were well matched. He hadn't been certain she would support his new business line, but her response had been immediately and overwhelmingly positive. He could only dream of having that in his life on a regular basis rather than just during a short visit a few times a year. Now that he knew what he was missing, it was only going to be worse.

He pressed on the speaker button and let it buzz on the other end for several seconds. He could have released it right away, but the irritating noise would let Michelle and his dad know that his patience was at an end.

"Hi, Daddy. Did you like your lunch?"

"It was tasty, but now it's time for Ginger to go home."

"What did you talk about? Are you going to go out on a date now?"

"Michelle!"

"But Dad—"

The speaker went silent for moment. Frank used that time to take a breath. When it clicked back on, Paul was the one speaking. "She's on her way to unlock the door. Remember that she's only nine. And that she loves you."

"I know you helped with this, Dad."

"Remember that I love you, too. Sorry about the entrée. She insisted."

"You should have known better. And I'm not talking about the Lunchables."

He cut the conversation when he saw his daughter through the window. She walked slowly but determinedly. Frank recognized the look she wore: the one that said she could do it herself, and she couldn't be told she was wrong. It was bad enough when she wore it during Phys. Ed. Class, trying to master one-handed cartwheels, or in math class arguing with her teacher about the need to show her work. He didn't want to see it when it came to his love life.

"Did you have a good time on your Christmas date?" she asked as soon as she stepped into the workshop.

"That wasn't a date, Michelle."

"But it was. You did a bunch of stuff together and then you ate. You even went dancing, and I didn't tell you to do that. How is that not a date?" she demanded.

"I didn't ask Ginger to do any of those things with me. And she didn't ask me."

"But you had a good time. I saw you."

His heart cracked when he saw her lip quiver. "I'm sorry, sweetheart, but you can't force people to go on a date just because you want them to."

Ginger crouched so she could look Michelle in the eye. "It's pretty special that you think your dad and I would be good dates for each other, but we talked about it over the summer and decided it wasn't something we both wanted. We can be friends without dating."

"Well, that's stupid. You should be boyfriend and girl-friend. Then you would be around a lot more and we'd all be happier. You two aren't working together right at all!" Michelle shouted at them.

His father must have anticipated this meltdown, because Paul came up behind Michelle before Frank could get to her. "Come on, little miss. Let's go have a chat. Ginger, always a pleasure. Thanks for being a good sport."

Ginger waited until the pair were back in the house. "I think this is my fault."

Frank stared at her, stunned. "How could this possibly be your fault?"

"Not the locking us in the workshop, but giving her the idea we should be dating."

"It's not—"

"I asked you out on a date. I didn't think to check where Michelle was when I put you on the spot. You said no, and I respect that. But if she did overhear us, then she might have gotten the wrong idea. If you think it will help, I can talk to her," Ginger offered.

"I promise this had nothing to do with her over-hearing you." If she had, she would have been unstop-pable. "Me dating again is a subject we've been discussing for a while."

"Either way, my presence is causing problems. If you want to request a new representative from North Pole Unlimited, I understand. Noel Berry is excellent. He specializes in the art section of the company's catalogue, and he'd be an excellent resource for your puzzle images."

Just when he thought the afternoon couldn't get any

worse, it hit a new depth. "I don't think that'll be necessary. I don't want to deal with anyone else." Then he realized what had been nagging him for the past two hours. "I hate to say this, after everything."

Ginger squared her shoulders. "Go ahead. I can handle it."

"We haven't discussed any of the business that brought you here today. You'd just come into the shop to say hi. You didn't bring your computer or briefcase or anything in from the car."

"I don't believe this." Then she darted to her car. Frank refused to drop his head in defeat, even if she were running for the hills. It had been an emotionally intense afternoon. He could give her time to get over their mutual embarrassment. They could always sign the paperwork she brought in the new year.

Then she came back, lugging her briefcase. "I forgot, too." She sounded like she wanted the afternoon to be over as badly as he did.

"Let's get down to the number crunching and details, then."

The brief, perfunctory conversation that followed was the most professional one Frank ever had with Ginger in his life. They discussed the contract amendments that Frank's lawyer and North Pole Unlimited's legal department had agreed on. They debated the pros and cons of the early plan the marketing team had put together for Catch Me If You Can. After he spent a few minutes on his hands and knees reconnecting the telephone and the Wi-Fi unit, Ginger called up the company's current selection of jigsaw puzzles, and they reviewed the limited but high-quality offerings, and noted where there were opportunities for Frank when he decided whether or not he was going to move ahead with his new project.

It was polite and productive and utterly impersonal. He'd never hated a business meeting more in his life.

Frank waited until she was done and putting away her computer. He couldn't take it anymore. "Ginger, what was the name of that fellow you said could take over for you?"

"Noel Berry. Why?"

"Because I think I'm going to need to talk to him."

CHAPTER 10

NOT EVEN DOUBLE-FUDGE cookies could calm this angry beast. Paul stood back and let Michelle stomp around the living room. She wasn't yelling anymore, or even speaking. She did stop to growl every few seconds, but he stayed silent and let her get it out of her system. Finally, she threw herself on the couch, pulled the crocheted blanket from the back, and dropped it over her like it could make her disappear. "Why are grown-ups so dense?" she asked.

"The older you get, the more complicated things get," Paul replied, knowing the truth wouldn't make her feel better.

"How complicated could it be? I don't understand why Dad and Ginger won't go out on a date. How much longer did it take you to ask Grandma out after she wrote her story? Months? Years?" she cried in frustration.

"Two days," he admitted. "But it felt longer."

It was two days after his crazy midnight ride, and the Christmas edition of the *Kenora Weekly Sentinel* was a huge hit. The whole town was reading it. The ghost reindeer spy for Santa was the talk of every donut shop and cashier counter in the area. If they hadn't known her name before, Molly Brown had become a household name and star reporter in the area. Everybody wanted to get to know her better.

Especially him.

Paul had stared in the mirror and given himself the pep talk of a lifetime, practicing what he wanted to say until he got the phrasing just right. Then he pulled on his black knit cap. Now he was in his truck on another scouting mission, but this time, his target was a certain brown-haired, brown-eyed reporter, and he was absolutely going to ask her out the next time he saw her.

Then he saw her.

He wasn't ready.

But she saw him, and it was too late to back out. Molly was wearing a red toque with a white pompom, and a thick red scarf around her neck. Her big, black leather mitts were full of grocery bags, and the camera around her neck bounced as she ran his way. "Did you see the paper?"

"Of course I saw the paper. I was looking for you to say congratulations on the front page."

Her smile was blinding. "My editor was absolutely thrilled with the shots. The story is being picked up across the country. It's running in the *Winnipeg Free Press* and the *Chronicle-Journal* in Thunder Bay today, and I'm getting full credit on the article and the photos."

"That's terrific."

"I have a reason to celebrate. Now I need someone to do it with."

He wasn't going to get a better opening than that. "How about me?"

Her head went back, and she blinked at him. Twice. "Excuse me?"

A hint of a smile played at the corner of her mouth. Paul knew she was going to make him say the words. Since he'd made her wait for them, he had it coming. "Would you like to go on a date with me sometime?"

"Sometime?"

Yep, she was definitely making him work for it. All that practicing in front of the mirror was about to pay off. "Molly Brown, would you go out for dinner with me at Lee's Chinese Restaurant at six o'clock tonight or on your next free evening?" Paul left nothing to chance: they'd already discussed their mutual love of wonton soup and ginger beef, six o'clock gave her time to get ready and still gave him long enough to eat before he had to start work for the night, and the option of another night meant that he intended to ask until he got a definitive answer.

She didn't make him work any harder than that because she gave him two responses immediately.

The first was a belly laugh.

The second was words. "It took you long enough."

After they'd made plans for dinner the next night—her office party was that night—he returned to his truck and sat idling at the curb. His hands shook from the adrenaline rush. After he replayed the conversation, he shook his head. Molly's enthusiastic acceptance had him wondering why he'd been worried in the first place.

"Of course, she said yes, Grandpa. Just like Ginger would if Dad asked, but he won't."

"That's not the point of the story, Michelle." She wasn't wrong, but he'd been trying to teach her that when Frank was ready, he would invite Ginger on a date, and no amount of encouragement, cajoling, or teasing would rush him.

Although Paul did wish his son would get on with it. Despite his and Michelle's voiced approval, he knew Frank was still hesitant about bringing a new woman into his life, and by extension, theirs. But Christmas was the season of miracles, so all he could do was hope his son wasn't going to blow the chance he and Michelle had so painstakingly provided.

CHAPTER 11

IF GINGER THOUGHT her heart had dropped the previous summer after Frank turned her down, the feeling she had now put it to shame. If Frank wanted a different representative, there would be no going back to their former easy camaraderie, no going forward with his new business plans, and no more visits to the Indie-Genius workshops.

She didn't blame him. She did regret his choice though. "I understand." If she ignored the personal devastation, she could try to concentrate on the professional disaster she'd caused. At least he wasn't leaving North Pole Unlimited altogether. She...

"Ginger!" Frank shouted, the exasperation in his voice evident.

Apparently, it wasn't the first time he'd tried to get her attention. She looked up and realized that at some point, Paul and Michelle had joined them in the workshop again. "Hi, sweetie. What, Frank? Don't worry, I—"

"I don't think you do," he said, interrupting her again. "Will you listen to me for a minute?"

"Of course." She could maintain her professionalism until she made her escape.

"I don't think that you should be my business contact if we're going to be dating. And I really hope we're going to be dating because I would like to go out with you. On a date. Many dates. Starting with lunch, the next time I visit December. Can I take you on a date to the Pumpkin Patch? That's the restaurant that has the soups you like, right?" He looked her straight in the eyes. "Ginger?"

The words sounded like English. Individually, she knew what they meant, but altogether they made no sense. "I don't understand."

"I'm asking you if you'd like to go out with me. In front of an audience. The asking part is in front of an audience. The date would be just the two of us," he clarified as he stared at his family.

"But you aren't interested. I asked you out over the summer."

"What can I say? I panicked."

That comment, matched with his smile, made the world click back into focus. It was such a Frank thing to say. Hope flickered in her chest. "You panicked because I asked you out?"

"Not because you asked me out. Because you suggested Troutman's Pier, and all I could think was that I didn't want either of us to get food poisoning. By the time I got my train of thought back on the tracks, you'd already left the province, and I couldn't think of a good way to bring it up again."

"Until I made you have your first date!" Michelle piped up from the door.

"So, no pressure, if you'd still like to try dating."

"Say yes, Ginger," Michelle added.

"Not helping, little miss," Frank said, his eyes not leaving Ginger's.

He looked so eager and anxious and earnest that Ginger knew without a doubt that he was already all in. So was she. "Totally helping, Michelle," she said with a laugh. "Yes, I'd love to go on a date with you, Frank."

"That's great." He didn't say anything else, but neither did she. They were too busy grinning at each other like idiots.

She didn't think about it, but out of the corner of her eye, she saw Paul lead Michelle out of the workshop, and heard him say, "Yep, just like his old man."

EPILOGUE

DECEMBER, *Manitoba*
  January 6ᵗʰ

"Delivery for Ms. Malone."

Ginger didn't look up from her computer screen. She was neck deep in recording holiday requests for the next three months, and she needed to get it done in the next fifteen minutes, because she couldn't be late for what was next on her schedule.

"Just put it over there, please." She blindly swung her arm out to point to a four-drawer cabinet in the corner. She knew the top of it was clear because she currently had all the files that were usually on it spread across her desk. She slapped a Post-it on Noel Berry's file, reminding him to check with the manufacturing department's deadlines when scheduling time off in the fall.

"I'd rather give it to you directly."

She looked up and was surprised to see the face grinning down at her. "Frank, you're here! And early. And bearing gifts!"

"We couldn't wait any longer."

She'd waited long enough, too.

After accepting Frank's invitation for a date back in mid-December, she'd returned to the office and begun the paperwork to transfer his account over to his new representative. Ginger was certain she could have kept working with Frank professionally, but if things progressed the way she hoped, it would become a conflict of interest, and she'd rather not have to worry about it later.

She and Frank had spoken almost every night since then. He'd kept her up to date about Michelle's last week of school before her winter break, and she'd kept him laughing with several stories of the last-minute insanity of trying to get hundreds of orders processed and delivered by Christmas Day. North Pole Unlimited had the process down to a fine art, but there were always monkey wrenches being thrown into the machine, like blizzards popping up despite predictions of clear skies, and a mislabeled batch of dye that was crimson instead of cyan, resulting in eight dozen bright pink toboggan mitts instead of blue ones.

She video-chatted with his whole family on Christmas and saw what Santa had brought to them courtesy of Michelle's show and tell. But she hadn't heard from Frank for over a week after that. He had taken Paul and Michelle to Hawaii on the twenty-sixth, and they'd spent a week exploring the tropical islands. Michelle had promised to send her a postcard, but she would be lucky to get it by Valentine's Day.

Now Frank and company were here in person. She knew Frank was meeting with Noel after their lunch date, but she hadn't expected Michelle and Paul to tag along. "What are you all doing here?" she asked.

"We're going to give you a souvenir from Maui, and then Ms. Lewis is going to take us to lunch in the cafeteria," Michelle said. "I can't wait to meet her in person." The little girl shoved a box of chocolate-covered macadamia nuts at her. "Here you go."

"Thank you."

Her small office got even more crowded when Jilly Lewis arrived. "Hurray, my guests are here. We're going to have lunch and then visit Veterinary Services. You two enjoy your extra-long lunch date." The three of them shuffled out of the office before Ginger had a chance to ask them a single question, like how they all managed to know each other.

"They didn't come all this way to eat at our cafeteria, did they?" Ginger asked as she pulled on her parka.

"No. We were in Winnipeg to check out the Granite Plains Academy for Michelle," Frank said. "They've got a really good program we think she'll enjoy next year. They have a huge computer lab and a full science lab. Plus, although she'll be one of the younger students there, she won't be the only student who's skipped a couple grades."

"Have you decided on boarding her in the school's residence, then?"

"No." He didn't elaborate until they were alone in her car on the way to the Pumpkin Patch. "We talked about it a lot while we were in Hawaii. If Michelle likes the school, we've decided to move to Winnipeg while she's a student. We'll be getting a house. Dad's going to stay in Kenora, and we'll go out there for holidays and summer vacation."

"That's..." She gulped. "That's a huge decision." One

that put him a lot closer to her. Over half the people who worked at North Pole Unlimited lived in the city and drove to December every day. Including her. It was only a half-hour trip. "Depending on where you decide you want to be, we could be neighbours."

"That's the hope."

Ginger hit the brakes hard as she pulled into the parking spot in front of the restaurant.

Frank placed his hand on top of hers on the gearshift and gave it a gentle squeeze. "I know that's an assumption on my part. But I have a strong feeling that this date is going to be the first of many, many, *many* more to come. I hope I'm not out of line saying that."

Ginger threw back her head and laughed. "Not at all. It's about time."

THE END

BONUS RECIPE: LEMON SQUARES

CRUST:

    1 cup butter (softened) or margarine
    1/2 cup confectioner's sugar
    1 1/2 cups all-purpose flour

FILLING:

    4 large eggs
    1 1/2 cups granulated sugar
    2 tsp fresh lemon zest
    1/2 cup freshly squeezed lemon juice
    1/4 cup all-purpose flour

Additional confectioner's sugar to sprinkle on top.

Preheat oven to 350F.

In a large mixing bowl, beat butter and confectioner's sugar until blended. Slowly beat in flour.

Press the dough into the bottom of a 9"x13" pan.

Bake 15 to 20 minutes until the edges are brown, like shortbread. Remove from oven. Leave oven on.

While the crust is baking, in a small bowl whisk eggs, granulated sugar, lemon zest, lemon juice, and flour until well combine. Pour it over the hot crust.

Return to oven and bake an additional 18-20 minutes until the top is light brown.

Cool completely. Dust the top with confectioner's sugar immediately before serving.

Cut into bars or squares. Refrigerate leftovers. (This doesn't freeze particularly well.)

MORE BOOKS FROM ELLE RUSH

SWEET CONTEMPORARY ROMANCE

<u>North Pole Unlimited</u>

Decker and Joy
Hollis and Ivy
Nick and Eve
Rudy and Kris
Ben and Jilly
Frank and Ginger

<u>North Pole Unlimited Collections</u>
(also available in paperback)

Collection 1 - Decker & Joy, Hollis & Ivy
Collection 2 - Nick & Eve, Rudy & Kris
Collection 3 - Ben & Jilly, Frank & Ginger

<u>Holiday Beach</u>
(also available in paperback)

Shamrocks and Surprises
Pumpkins and Promises
Tinsel and Teacups
Fireworks and Frenemies

Hopewell Millionaires

Doctor Millionaire
Fall a Million Times
A Million Love Notes

Royal Oak Ranch

The Cowboy and the Movie Star
The Cowboy and the Pastry Princess
The Cowboy and the Constable

Resort Romances

Cuban Moon
Mexican Sunsets
Dominican Stars
Mayan Midnights
Complete series 4-book box set

COOKBOOKS

Heartmade Collection

Brunch
Mains and Sides
Holiday Table

ABOUT THE AUTHOR

ELLE RUSH IS a sweet contemporary romance author from Winnipeg, Manitoba, Canada. When she's not travelling, she's hard at work writing books which are set all over the world. From Hollywood to the house next door, her heroes will make you sigh, and her heroines will make you laugh out loud.

Elle has a degree in Spanish and French, barely passed German, and is learning Italian. She flunked poetry in every language she ever studied. She also has mild addictions to tea, yarn, terrible sci-fi movies, and home renovation shows.

To keep up with news and upcoming releases, sign up for her newsletter at **www.ellerush.com/newsletter**.